Miriam can scarcely believe how Gideon and his brothers are caring for her motherless nieces.

"At first, I could scarcely credit it, but then I took stock of the clothing, and I realized my niece was wearing the only dress she owns! Pardon me if I'm drawing the wrong conclusion, but as far as I can tell, you men let that little girl run about in a man's shirt. How could you allow such a travesty?"

"Travesty? It's no travesty. Bryce and Logan outgrew those shirts. It's shameful to waste."

"Shameful! Why, you cannot mean—"

"They serve Polly just fine." Gideon glowered at her. "Besides, who's going to see her but us, anyhow?"

His assertions left her spluttering. The matter was far from closed in her opinion. He wasn't about to have her dictate his family's ways; she refused to leave her sweet little nieces alone with a band of barely civilized men. He folded his arms akimbo.

"Best you forget these opinions and wild notions about staying, Miss Miriam. For the next few days, you'd do well to rest. You're looking peaked, and that won't make for a very good voyage."

"Voyage?"

"Home," he asserted. His head nodded, as if to paint an exclamation mark in the air to punctuate his feelings. "We'll just trade in your return ticket for an earlier departure."

CATHY MARIE HAKE is a Southern California native who loves her work as a nurse and Lamaze teacher. She and her husband have a daughter, a son, and two dogs, so life is never dull or quiet. Cathy considers herself a sentimental packrat, collecting antiques and Hummel figurines. In spare moments, she reads, bargain hunts, and makes a huge mess with her new hobby of scrapbooking. E-mail Cathy at: cathy@cathymariehake.com

Books by Cathy Marie Hake

HEARTSONG PRESENTS

HP370—Twin Victories
HP481—Unexpected Delivery
HP512—Precious Burdens
HP545—Love Is Patient
HP563—Redeemed Hearts
HP583—Ramshackle Rose
HP600—Restoration

One Chance in a Million

Cathy Marie Hake

Heartsong Presents

To Kelly and Tracey, because you're so fun to brainstorm with. To Tracie for her enthusiasm, and to Christian sisters everywhere who make mission fields of their homes and let their lights shine for the Lord.

A note from the Author:
I love to hear from my readers! You may correspond with me by writing:

Cathy Marie Hake
Author Relations
PO Box 719
Uhrichsville, OH 44683

ISBN 1-59310-192-9

ONE CHANCE IN A MILLION

Our mission is to publish and distribute inspirational products offering exceptional value and biblical encouragement to the masses.

All scripture quotations are taken from the King James Version of the Bible.

PRINTED IN THE U.S.A.

Or check out our Web site at www.heartsongpresents.com

one

"Stand back, else I'll make ye shark bait."

Miriam Hancock suppressed a shudder and shuffled backward to give the seaman space. He had plenty of room to get past her, even with his rolling gait. He and the other men sailing the vessel were more than ready to do her ill. She'd done nothing to deserve their wrath, but they'd served it up in large portions ever since the *Destiny* set sail.

Another crewman clamped his hand around her elbow. "I'll help you down the plank."

She fought the urge to yank away. Within the first days of the voyage from the islands to San Francisco, Miriam had found it necessary to push away overly familiar hands and use her hatpin to counter unwanted advances. Twice she'd been accosted by men who had gotten into her cabin. Both times, she'd managed to save her virtue; but the captain, needing to safeguard her and prevent incipient mutiny, took to locking her in her cabin.

The *Destiny* had finally docked. Today was the first time in weeks she'd been on deck.

"Here. I'll carry that." The rough seaman grabbed the valise from Miriam's numb fingers and hauled her toward a gangplank. The splintered length of wood looked anything but safe. His steadying hold would keep her balanced if she cooperated. Truth be told, the way the gangplank seesawed

5

between ship and dock, the most able assistance might not be sufficient.

A wry smile twisted her lips. Even now, she still might become shark bait.

Once she reached the dock, Miriam fought to stay upright.

"You've lost yer landlegs," her escort chortled. He seemed oblivious to the fact that he had no business mentioning lower limbs to a woman of decency. "Stand here a bit. I heard you have a slip o' paper 'bout where to go." He leaned closer and jabbed his calloused thumb at his chest. His rotten teeth made for fetid breath. "You could lose that paper an' wait fer Jake O'Leary. I'll be on shore leave in nigh unto an hour. I could show you a right fine time."

She snatched her valise from him. Before she could say anything, someone barked, "O'Leary!"

The sailor jolted to attention. "Aye, Cap'n?"

Captain Raithly stalked down the gangplank. "I'll see to the lady." He pried the valise from Miriam and braced her arm as he led her off the dock. "I did my best by you. You have to understand that."

"It was a difficult voyage."

"Aye." Within a quarter hour, he'd hired a beefy shoreman to heft her two trunks to the street. From there, she took a hansom cab to the address Captain Raithly gave the driver. Already weary, she relied upon the skill of the mercantile's owner to arrange the next leg of her journey. Miriam ardently hoped he'd suggest she spend a night at one of the local boardinghouses before he sent her along, but as luck would have it, a stage was ready to leave and there was room on it for her.

By the time the stage stopped in Reliable, Miriam was perilously close to tears. She stood in the street of the tiny town, steamer trunks at her side, as a chilly breeze swirled dirt about her and twilight warned she'd best find shelter. She looked around. Despair welled up. She saw only two women in the whole of the town. Neither could be mistaken for a lady.

Men abounded. They assessed her with more than polite glances. She'd been subjected to far too many leers to be innocent of the lurid intent behind such looks. To her mortification, Miriam knew she was a spectacle. She hurriedly searched up and down the street to spot the local boardinghouse. She desperately needed a fresh bed and a solid night's sleep.

Just as she came to the dismaying conclusion that no boardinghouse existed, a brick wall of a man burst through the place across the street. The batwing saloon doors banged wide open, and he held two adolescents by their ears. Both scrambled to match his stride, and from the looks on their faces, they'd do a jig to keep up so he'd not pinch any harder. The smaller one whined, "Only two beers, Gideon!"

"Neither of you has any business in there," the man growled.

"C'mon, Gideon," the older protested, "I'm fifteen!"

The brick wall hauled them to horses hitched directly to Miriam's left. "Fifteen and foolish," he said. "If you ever sneak off and try a stunt like this again, I'll tan your hides 'til you can't sit."

The younger of the two lads seemed a bit loose limbed. Gideon grabbed him and half-tossed him into his saddle. He took the fifteen-year-old by the back of his trousers and gave him a very uncomfortable-looking boost onto his mount. He unhitched all three horses, and as Gideon mounted his own gelding, the first boy mishandled his reins. His horse danced sideways until his hindquarters swung around. The

youngster lost his balance and fell right out of the saddle—
onto Miriam.

Miriam watched in astonishment as the horse's hindquarters
came close. She'd stepped back and twisted, but her steamer
trunks blocked any further escape. When the boy slumped and
slid toward her, she let out a breathless yelp and tried to right
him, but he didn't help in the least. He hit her with just
enough force and weight to rob her of her balance.

Oomphf! Air whooshed out of her lungs as she landed flat
on her back on a trunk. The considerable weight of the youth
sandwiched her there.

"Whoopie!" he shouted as he clumsily wrapped his arms
about her, then tried to nuzzle her neck.

Miriam kicked and shoved. Instead of dislodging him, she
only managed to cause them both to roll off the trunk and
onto the filthy street. He held her fast as they tumbled 'round
one more time. Her head hit something hard. Just as nausea
and panic welled up, Miriam felt the weight lifted off her.
Through pain-narrowed eyes, she watched the brick wall
shake the kid.

"Logan, behave yourself for a change." He flung the kid
away and hunkered down. "Ma'am? Are you all right?"

She lay there, still unable to draw air back into her lungs.
Her head hurt something fierce. She closed her eyes and gritted her teeth.

A rough hand cupped her jaw. "Ma'am? Logan, you brained
her!"

"Schee's re—al purdy, Gideon. Kin I keep her?"

"Drunken fool," Gideon muttered as he tunneled his arms
beneath her. Miriam heard him from a great distance and felt
the world tumble into a cold, dizzying swirl.

The next thing she knew, Miriam roused to find herself

draped across a strange man's lap. A host of tattered-looking men encircled them, and a good half-dozen lanterns illuminated her less-than-circumspect situation. Pain and mortification wrung a moan out of her, and her lashes dropped a mere second after they'd lifted.

"She's comin' 'round," someone observed.

The man who held her cupped her head to his shoulder and ordered in a quiet tone that carried exceptionally well, "You men mosey on back to your own business. This gal isn't going to want to be crowded. She needs breathing room."

"Whatcha gonna do if your kid brother addled her wits?"

"I doubt her wits are addled," he gritted.

Miriam dimly wondered if she ought to thank him for his faith in her or if she ought to be angry that he'd made such a pronouncement without first checking with her. She hadn't even begun to evaluate the damage done yet. Her head felt abominable and her stomach roiled. She drew in a slow breath to steady herself and push away the pain. A rough thumb brushed lightly back and forth across her cheekbone. Oddly enough, it comforted her.

"All right, sweet pea, open your eyes again. Look at me and say your head doesn't hurt too bad."

She slowly lifted her lashes and stared up into a pair of bright blue, concerned eyes. Three lines furrowed his forehead. Clearly he was worried about her. A flicker of warmth stole across her soul. A lock of black, wavy hair fell onto his forehead. He impatiently shook it back out of the way and gently combed his fingers through the loosened mess that had once been her modest, practical coiffure. His fingers hit a spot behind her ear, and she sucked in a sharp breath. The darkness started to swirl around her all over again.

He moaned. "Sorry. You've got a nasty goose egg there."

His rough hand curled around the nape of her neck and gently kneaded. "Just give yourself a minute here."

A minute. Oh, it was going to take far more than a paltry minute for her to feel decent again. She shivered partly from cold, partly from pain, and mostly because she'd never had a man hold her like this. Miriam closed her eyes and fought the urge to burrow closer to the stranger. She felt miserable, afraid, and lonely, and she never knew being held in the arms of a behemoth could be so comforting.

"Hey, now, Bryce. The little lady's starting to shiver. Get my bedroll." A second later, he lifted and slipped her into the folds of something thick and a bit scratchy that carried the scent of wood smoke. Solicitude the likes of which she'd never known surfaced. He gallantly wrapped her, then tucked the edges of the blanket around her throat.

Was it the instant warmth of the blanket or the deft way he held and enveloped her that let her lie limp in his arms? She moved her head ever so slightly, and pain streaked from nape to temple. Pain. Definitely pain was the culprit in her unladylike place of repose.

"This'll help, ma'am." He didn't act at all as if this were an unusual circumstance or one worthy of alarm. He kept his deep voice pitched low and calming. "Why don't you tell me your name and where you're bound? I'll send for someone to come fetch you."

She wet her lips and whispered, "I'm Miriam Hancock. I'm here to help my sister."

"Your sister?" His voice sounded a bit strained. "Who is she?"

"Hannah Chance."

The arms holding her tightened.

two

She peeled her eyes open. "Do you know her?"

"Yes."

Several of the bystanders murmured, but Miriam couldn't distinguish what they said. Her head pounded like a marching band. She slipped her hand out of the blanket and cupped it over the part of her head that felt so awful. "Perhaps, if it wouldn't be too much trouble, you could ask her husband, Daniel, to come fetch me."

"Miss Miriam, there's no need." He paused and said very quietly, "Daniel is my brother."

"Which one are you?"

"Gideon." Before she could ask about her sister, he said, "Don't say another word, Miss Miriam. Rely on me. I'll take you home."

"The Lord works in mysterious ways," she whispered.

"Shh. Best you go on and sleep through your headache."

"Hannah—what did she have?"

"A girl. She's a darlin' little thing."

She sighed, but her lips bowed upward. Just as she opened them to ask more, Gideon ordered, "No more questions, Miss Miriam. If you're fretting about your things, let me put your mind at ease. We don't have a wagon, so your trunks can stay at the livery tonight. The owner there is a friend of mine, so I can guarantee everything will be safe."

He stood and handed her off to someone. Miriam barely muffled her whimper at the loss of his comforting strength.

"Hand her back. Careful."

The man holding her lifted her high, and suddenly the world that already felt unsteady began to spin. Miriam let out a small cry.

"Here we go, sweet pea." To her relief, she ended up in Gideon's arms again. "I mean no disrespect, but I aim to hold you close."

She didn't know what the proper response to such a comment should be, and she couldn't think well enough to concoct a reply. Her head hurt too much.

"Bryce, you see to it Miss Hancock's trunks are taken care of. Then do what you need to, to make sure Logan stays on his horse and gets home. Bring Miss Hancock's valise."

It seemed as if they rode forever. Miriam's head pounded, and Gideon seemed to understand she couldn't summon the strength to be sociable. He held her securely, and she abandoned any hope of sitting properly. He made no comment about how she draped limply across his lap like seaweed. In fact, every once in a while, he'd give her a soothing stroke as if she weren't a bother at all. The beat of his heart was the only sound between them, and for some reason, the steady rhythm lulled her just as invitingly as the constant surf she'd heard from her bedroom window back home. The drowsiness she felt was a blessing—it kept the nausea at bay.

His order for her to remain silent could be considered a veritable godsend. Miriam knew she'd embarrass herself if she had to carry on much of a conversation. Even if the queasiness waned, her thoughts scattered too hopelessly for her to stay coherent. She finally tilted her face up to his and whispered, "I don't mean to be impatient, but is it much farther?"

"We're traveling at a walk. Too many gopher holes. I can't

risk having Splotch break a leg. It's a solid hour more. Need me to stop for you to, um, take care of, ah, business?"

Though chagrined, she confessed, "I'd be most appreciative."

He eased her forward, then his solid torso crowded her for a moment as he leaned with the action of swinging out of the saddle. The whole while, his hands stayed clamped securely about her waist. Once he was on the ground, he slid her off the horse.

Her first impression couldn't have been more accurate. This close, there could be no denying the fact that Gideon Chance was a brick wall. He towered over her, and her feet hadn't even touched earth yet. When he set her down, she was anything but steady. Concern colored his voice as he braced her. "I'm going to turn us back to town after you're done. This isn't right."

"Land. Not used to it. The ship. . ."

"Ahh." A wealth of understanding and relief filled that single syllable as he drew it out.

When they got underway again, he smoothed the blanket around her, dipped his head, and said in a quiet rumble, "I want you to go ahead and sleep now. No use in sitting here hurting if you can drowse through the pain."

"You're most understanding." She tried to hide her yawn, but from his smile, she knew he'd caught her at it. The way he nestled her a tad closer caused an extraordinary sense of security to wash over her. For weeks, she'd lived in dread of every man aboard the *Destiny*. Though she'd just met him, she had an innate sense she could trust Gideon Chance. Besides, Hannah said he was a fine man. Miriam let her heavy lids drift shut and left herself in capable, caring arms.

Gideon watched sleep overtake her and let out a sigh of relief. He'd managed to keep her from asking any questions yet. He tried to figure out what to do. Things were going to be a mite bit sticky for a while.

He'd taken the closest horse when he left the ranch in such a fit. The snappy little paint carried him well, but it was a good thing Hannah's sister was a tiny woman. Gideon didn't believe in pushing an animal too hard. If only he could train up his kid brothers as well as he'd tamed Splotch. . . .

His brothers rode up. Bryce showed the good judgment of letting their horses travel at a mere walk, too—in part to keep Logan upright but also out of caution. Still, since Gideon had stopped along the way for Miriam, they'd made up for the time spent hauling her trunks to the livery.

"Whatcha going to do with her?" Bryce asked.

"We'll see."

"Didja tell her yet?"

He glanced down to be sure she still slept. "No."

"Why not?"

Gideon glared at his brother. "Because her head hurts, you dolt." Bryce could make animals do anything he wanted with a mere look and gesture, but when it came to people, he never seemed to quite comprehend the finer points. Most of the time, it didn't much matter, but tonight, Gideon had spent his patience.

"I'm sorry, Gideon," Logan mumbled. The brisk air helped sober him up a bit.

"You'd better be sorry. If I ever catch you going into the Nugget again before you're a full-grown man, I'll make you wish you'd never been born." He then turned his attention toward his other brother. "And I hold you accountable, Bryce. What were you thinking, taking him in there?"

"Well, I was thinkin' on how pretty Lulabell—"

"Hush!" Gideon hastily assured himself the woman in his

arms hadn't heard his brother's confession. Bad enough, she knew they'd been far too liberal with libations. The last thing he needed was an unmarried missionary's daughter to find out the second-to-the-youngest Chance male foolishly had just tried to visit a house of ill repute.

Hannah would have pitched an ever-lovin' hissy fit over Bryce and Logan's trip to the Nugget. As it was, she'd made her disapproval clear on the rare occasions when the older brothers bent an elbow. They'd all tried to shield her from their forays to the saloon by chewing a few sprigs of mint on the way home to disguise the smell of the single mug of beer they'd indulged in. Inevitably, when their ploy failed, Daniel managed to cajole her into masking her scorn for their sinful indulgence when "thirst got the better of their judgment."

Only now, Daniel wouldn't hold any sway with Miriam. No doubt, she'd be every bit as priggish as her sister. Under his breath, Gideon muttered a desperate man's prayer, "Heaven help me. I'm not up to dealing with all of this."

He studied her a bit more. Her eyes had been murky green, but he wasn't certain whether pain caused that. Then again, from the shadows beneath her eyes, it could well be from weariness, too. She'd traveled a long way. Her skin looked fair as could be, and that made no sense since she'd been living in the tropics. When Daniel brought Hannah home, her skin held a bit of sun bronzing. Her hair had been moonlight pale, but this woman's carried a warm golden cast.

He'd need to get her a new bonnet. The one she'd been wearing got knocked off in the mishap, and the gelding managed to relieve himself on the ugly creation before it could be rescued. To Gideon's way of thinking, Knothead probably judged the haberdasher's nightmare and did that as a declaration of his opinion. Secretly, he counted the ruination of such a homely concoction of straw and flowers no great loss. *In fact, Knothead did Miriam a favor by destroying it.*

Miriam Hancock looked much like her sister. At best, she could be considered a small dab of a gal—and Hannah's frailty proved to be problematic. Ranch life had been too harsh for her. Gideon often considered her to be an exotic orchid, but only weeds and wildflowers survived this rugged land. Hannah barely made it past the second birthing in three years and finally succumbed to what an itinerant, self-professed sawbones diagnosed as "the punies."

When Miriam woke, he was going to have to tell her she'd traveled all of this way in vain. He didn't relish the notion of breaking the news. As the eldest, the unpleasant responsibility fell on his shoulders.

They rode along in near silence. Gideon got to thinking it was a crying shame Miriam didn't feel a far sight better. She'd undoubtedly agree with him that nothing on earth could match the sheer beauty of this slice of land. The sky looked close enough to touch, and the light breeze carried a refreshing, brisk pine scent. As she slept, little Miriam missed the crickets' song, too. He might not be one of those Bible-thumpin' men, but moments like these let him know God was God, and man owed Him his thanks.

When they reached the ranch, Bryce reined in his gelding and shifted in his saddle. "You gonna wake up Daniel so she can go stay with him?"

Three years ago, when Daniel got back, the brothers were glad to see him, but the surprise of him having a bride—let alone a preacher's daughter he'd snagged in the islands—set things awry. They'd been without Mama almost a year before Dan originally left, and most of the civilized niceties had fallen by the wayside in the intervening months. Hannah made Daniel a happy man, so his brothers all tried their best to change things to suit her. They even pitched in together and built the newlyweds their own little place so they'd have a bit of privacy.

Gideon cast a glance at the tiny cottage off to the side of the main house. He couldn't see a flicker of a lamp, so he shook his head. "Daniel's got the girls to sleep already. Go on in and hang a blanket between my bed and the rest. She can use my bunk tonight."

Bryce tromped in. Titus came out and raised his brows at the load Gideon nestled on his lap. He shook his head in disbelief, then paced off to the stable. A moment later, he passed by with a fistful of nails and a hammer. Within a few minutes, the sound of their work ceased. Gideon waited outside until they were done. The last thing Miriam needed was to hear a bunch of hammering. Judging from the lump on her head, she'd suffer a beaut of a headache for a few days. Titus came out. "It's ready. I pulled back your blanket."

Gideon nodded acknowledgment. He walked across the plank floor and asked, "Where is her valise?"

"Next to the bed," Paul said. He plopped down on the bench and stared at Miss Hancock as if he'd never seen a woman. Sad truth was, it had been a long while since he'd set eyes on a decent one.

Once behind the makeshift partition his brothers made by hanging a moth-eaten blanket from the ceiling joist, Gideon laid his feminine burden on the bed. His nose wrinkled. Come morning, she was going to be one very unhappy lady. Logan managed to roll her over toward the hitching post, and she'd gotten what polite women called "road apple" ground into her gown, petticoats, and stockings. She'd be mortified if she ever found out her skirts had been in a froth clear up to her knees. He made a mental note to threaten his brothers with dire punishment if they ever dared to mention that embarrassing fact.

His lips thinned. There was no way around it. She had to get out of these clothes. Feeling less than gallant, Gideon unbuckled her valise and peered inside. He fished about and found a nightdress. Now, he had to get her into it.

His hands started to sweat. It nearly undid him, just handling that oh-so-white, soft-from-a-hundred-washings bedgown. She'd embroidered flowers and tatted a tiny row of lace along the neckline, making the simple piece captivatingly, impossibly feminine. If that wasn't bad enough, it smelled like sunshine and honeysuckle. He abruptly set the piece on the foot of the bed. He had no business seeing her unmentionables or touching them.

Gideon tried to pet her cheek and coax her to rouse, but she slept on. He whispered a prayer for strength. Bad enough he'd seen and touched her light-as-air nightdress. Worse, now, he'd have to help her if she didn't wake up right quick.

"Come on, Miriam. Open your eyes, just for a few minutes," he said a bit more forcefully. She gave no response. He decided to take off her shoes. Maybe that would wake her up. After carefully lifting the hem of her truly ugly brown serge dress a scant few inches, he unbuttoned her tiny black leathers from ankle top to instep. With a quick twist and yank, he divested her of the footwear.

Less than eager to glide his hands up her stockinged calves, he took the toe of her left black lisle stocking and pulled. He met with some resistance, so he gingerly pinched both sides of the ankles and tugged. To his infinite relief, the garters yielded and he pulled off the stocking. By the time he got the other stocking off, he felt like he had a fever. Looking at Miss

Miriam's trim, lily-white ankles was enough to make a man loco.

His voice sounded hoarse as he tried once more to summon her from her sleepy world. "Miriam, wake up."

The woman didn't even flicker an eyelash.

He couldn't very well leave her to sleep in her badly soiled day gown. Gideon gritted his teeth against a rush of sensations as he reached out and unfastened the first button at her throat. The dress had twenty-eight tiny mother-of-pearl buttons aligned in disciplined ranks, two by two down the front. He stood there and prayed if he loosened the first pair, Miriam would come awake. Undoing one practically drained him of whatever control he possessed. He certainly couldn't handle twenty-seven more.

Heaven must have heard him, because he learned in the next instant that only half of those buttons needed to be undone; the other half were decorative companions. He'd just undone the second one and grimaced. She still hadn't roused. Bad enough, he'd had to loosen her clothes—she'd be utterly scandalized if she awoke to him dragging a wet cloth over her throat to rouse her. Gideon rested his hands on her shoulders, but he didn't want to shake her or shout. Poor thing didn't deserve that. He leaned closer and opened his mouth to whisper her name.

three

Miriam came awake with a vengeance. A cry burst from her as she catapulted into a sitting position. She windmilled her arms and whacked Gideon in the chest and jaw. For a wee bit of a thing, she sure showed spunk. Titus, Paul, Bryce, and Logan all scrambled over to see what the ruckus was about. When she spied them, Miriam let out a terrified shriek and tried to bolt from the far side of the bed.

Gideon did the most expedient thing. He grabbed the blanket and yanked it shut again, effectively containing and covering her. "Calm down." He sat down and pulled her back into his lap. "Everything is fine, sweet pea. Don't bother with them. They're leaving. You nitwits get on outta here before I knock your heads together."

"Oh, Lord, have mercy," she quavered. "Deliver me, I pray."

Gideon crooked his forefinger and used it to tilt her face up to his. Her eyes were wide with terror. "Hush, Miss Miriam. You don't have a thing in the world to fret over when it comes to me and the boys. You've got my ironclad guarantee on it. When you took your tumble in town, you got some, uh, stuff on your day gown. I tried to wake you a bit, but you're a sound sleeper."

She continued to shiver in his arms and stared at him in abject fear. White, even teeth clamped down hard on her lip, and he knew she did it to keep from screaming. Her breaths came in sharp little pants, causing her whole body to jerk.

He slowly smoothed a few errant strands of hair from her

brow. "How's your head feeling?" he asked softly, trying to divert her attention and let her gather her composure.

"Please don't hurt me. Don't touch me. Just let me go." She tacked on for good measure, "It's a sin."

"Sweet pea, nobody's planning to hurt you one bit. I'm sorry you got so spooked, but you don't have a worry in the world when it comes to that sinning business. I won't abide any man accosting a woman." He trailed his fingers down her cold, pale cheek. Brave as could be, she'd not shed any of the tears glistening in her huge eyes. Her skin felt soft as baby Virginia's. At the moment, she looked almost as young and innocent as little Ginny, too.

She managed to tear her gaze from his only long enough to hastily scan the room. The instant she refocused on him, she swallowed hard. "Where's Hannah?"

Gideon bit back a groan. He'd wanted to delay this.

"Saints have mercy," she whispered in a breathless rush. Eyes huge and swimming, she said, "You're not really Gideon, are you? If you were, Hannah would be here."

"Easy now, Miss Miriam. Easy." His arms tightened a shade. "I'm Gideon. Don't go letting your imagination lead you into unfounded fears."

"Then where is my sister?" Even though the volume had to make her head hurt, Miriam raised her shaking voice. "Hannah? Hannah!"

Gideon gently pressed a finger over her lips. "Hannah isn't coming, Miss Miriam."

"Why not?"

The whole way home, he'd tried to put together a few mild phrases that would gradually ease her into the sad truth. Maybe not something flowery, but well. . .

For all his pondering, he'd concocted a hundred phrases,

but none of them seemed right. The time had come, and he still lacked the words.

Gideon's momentary hesitation was all it took. Miriam went rigid in his arms. One of her hands snaked out from beneath the flap in the blanket and desperately clutched at his shirtfront. "No!"

He sighed and drew her closer. Gliding his palm up and down her back, Gideon confirmed her suspicion. "I'm afraid so, Miss Miriam. Hannah passed on soon after having little Virginia Mae. You must not have gotten Daniel's letter."

She burrowed her face in his neck and shook her head. Gideon wasn't sure whether she shook to deny the death or because she hadn't gotten the letter. He'd shocked her so deeply, he knew she'd not cry yet. In time, it would all register. For now, the shock protected her a shade. Gideon knew his words would echo and elicit a full reaction later.

Boots scuffled, and Paul appeared. He thrust a glass into Gideon's hand. It held water, but a telltale sweet odor clung to it. Paul mouthed, "Laudanum," and his brother gratefully accepted it.

It took some coaxing to get Miriam to drink it. She swallowed the first few sips out of shocked compliance, but when she realized the cup didn't contain plain water, she'd tried to refuse more. Gideon used all of his persuasive powers, and finally she finished the rest of the glass. The dull grief on her face was all too familiar. Daniel still wore it much of the time.

She eventually pushed away from him and said in a shaky voice, "I thank you for your honesty. H–Hannah mentioned you and your brothers in the most complimentary way in her missives. Now perhaps you would be so kind as to take me to her gravesite."

"I'll be willing to take you there, come morning. It's real late.

You need to go to bed."

"But I came to see Hannah."

The bewildered, lost look on her face tugged at his heart. "Sweet pea, you'll have to trust me. I'll take you to pay your respects tomorrow—first thing in the morning, if you like. Right now, you need to lie down." He patted her bedgown so she would focus on it. "If I leave you for a few minutes, can you change into this all by yourself?"

She nodded.

He stood and set her on her feet. After assuring himself that she could balance, he slowly let go. "About your clothes, just drop them on the blanket."

"Very well."

He moved her nightgown so she could reach it more easily. Even that fleeting contact left his fingertips burning. He cleared his throat. "Soon as you're changed, climb on into the bed."

Gideon left her and tried to ignore the sound of rustling clothes and the whisper of petticoats. He and his brothers waited in vain for the muffled crackling sound of her settling on his hay mattress. Finally he shrugged and drew closer to the blanket curtain. He quietly murmured her name, but she didn't answer, so he stepped back onto the other side of the makeshift partition.

His heart twisted. Miriam looked like a little angel, dressed in her pure white nightgown. She'd fallen asleep while kneeling to pray. Instead of being confined in the prim bun that had been coming loose all evening, her hair now hung in a loose braid that measured the full length of her spine. Her back bowed from the way her arms winged out onto the mattress, and she rested her cheek on one small, dainty hand.

He tiptoed over and winced at the noise his boots made on

the gritty plank floor. Thankfully she didn't jar awake again. The poor woman couldn't possibly withstand another shock. Gideon gently scooped her into his arms. For a moment, he held her close.

Other than Mama, he couldn't remember ever holding a woman just because she needed tenderness. Oh, he cherished his nieces, but they were tiny little scraps—not full-grown women. Miriam's head rested on his shoulder, and even in her slumber, she let out a tiny whimper.

"Shh," he murmured. "Sleep, darlin'. Just sleep." As he did when Polly or Ginny Mae were a bit fractious, he dipped one shoulder to the side, then the other to make his torso rock. For some odd reason, that swaying action always calmed them down. It worked for Miriam, too. After a minute or so, her features softened, and she let out a tiny puff of air.

"There you go," he whispered, then slipped her onto his bed and pulled up the wool blanket he normally used. Coarse. The blanket felt much too rough for a lady, but he figured she was too far gone to let a detail like that register tonight. In the morning, he'd rummage through a trunk and see if he could find one of Mama's quilts. Hannah took a shine to them, so her sister would probably appreciate having one to use while she visited.

Miriam turned her head to the side. The gentle curve of her jaw and the slight lift of her brow made him think an angel must have just whispered a word of comfort to her. Unable to resist, he bent down and brushed a chaste kiss on her cheek. . . just in case the angel hadn't done a good enough job.

After he straightened up, he cast a quick look over at the partition. Relief flooded him. None of his brothers was peeking around the blanket, so no one witnessed him pampering this strange woman. Even though he'd meant nothing personal or improper, he'd have to watch his ways for the time Miriam stayed here. He didn't want her—or his brothers—getting any crazy notions.

Gideon gathered the soiled blanket and clothes from the floor and noted she'd been orderly enough to fold each garment. A wry smile tilted his mouth. She'd tried to observe all propriety by placing her dress atop the pile so the men wouldn't see her unmentionables. Something was missing, though. Then, he spied a white length of cording hanging below the blanket at the foot of the bed. Prissy little Miriam had hidden her corset from him.

&

Much as it embarrassed her, Miriam had no choice. Someone had carried away all of her proper clothes. She'd need to traipse about in her nightgown and robe until her dress or trunks reappeared. Her head ached, but the sharp pangs of grief in her heart rated more attention. She brushed and put up her hair, pulled on the jade green robe, and tiptoed past the hanging blanket.

The sight before her almost felled her. Four other beds stuck out from the wall. Clothes hung from pegs pounded into the rugged wood walls, but more littered the mud-encrusted floor. Though it wasn't exactly the height of good manners to gawk at anyone—especially someone of the opposite gender—as they slept, she couldn't help noting each bed held a strapping man and a single blanket. No sheets were in sight.

Her bare feet made no noise, but they seemed to find every dirt clod and pebble on the floor as she made her way past the beds and out the open door. She closed the door behind herself and stifled a gasp.

A big trestle table flanked by benches filled the middle portion of the house. As she got closer, Miriam quelled a shriek as a mouse skittered by. The table hadn't been scrubbed in months. A sputtering candle sat in the center of it. Any number of items littered the floor, too. A harness, work gloves, a whetstone, and two saddles all blocked her transit. The windows were dingy beyond belief, and no curtain hung there for the sake of modesty or privacy.

Worst of all, the kitchen would make any woman's heart fail. A big Acme stove promised sizable meals, but a fleeting touch confirmed it to be stone cold and in desperate need of scraping and scouring. She peered into the water reservoir and almost screamed when she found two trout there. Crates nailed to the walls held provender. The Chance men might not clean at all, but from the looks of the supplies they kept, they certainly ate. Dirty dishes lay on every available surface.

Miriam cringed, then used the edge of a dubious-looking dishcloth to wipe a tiny circle on the windowpane until she could see. It was still dark outside. She couldn't determine the time. Regardless, she couldn't go back to sleep.

She used the candle to light a kerosene lamp and set to work. It was hard to determine where to begin. A quick touch of the broom handle, and she drew back in disgust. Sticky. She wiped it clean, then brandished the business end against the cobwebs in the corners. The overhead beams and walls soon were whisked clean, too. Next, she filled a bucket with water from the pump and relocated the fish into it.

It made no sense to try to suds down the stove until she scraped off the worst of the grime with the blade of a hoe she found on a bench. Though it wasn't exactly the usual application for the tool, the inside of a house wasn't a normal storage place for it, either. The hoe also helped her shovel the mountain of ashes from the stove. She set the buckets of ashes off to the side. They might be needed to make soap.

A bottle of ammonia allowed her to scrub the top of the range and the bottom panes of the windows. She couldn't reach the higher ones until she dragged over a bench, but with all of the rubbish in the way, she simply couldn't. Miriam pretended not to notice how the bowl stuck to the tabletop as she mixed flour, salt, baking powder, water, and eggs together in it. She'd set a small fire in the stove and would make some drop biscuits as soon as she heard the men begin to stir.

The coffeepot looked battered, but that indicated these men liked the bitter brew, so she refilled it with fresh water and measured out the grounds. Miriam put the coffee on the stove, and as she turned around, she bit back a cry. A pot holder she'd quilted for her sister hung on a rusty nail. Memories flooded her. All of the grief she'd tried to hold at bay with her frantic cleaning overwhelmed her. She hugged the pot holder to her bosom, sat at the sticky table, and wept.

four

Gideon had gone out to the stable to sleep. He woke to answer the call of nature, and on the way back to the stable from the outhouse, he noted the light from the house. That struck him as odd. The lights normally didn't show much at all. His brothers must be up trying to comfort little Miriam for the place to be ablaze like this. It was a solid half hour before they normally got up, and all of them prized their sleep. Things must be bad if they sacrificed their time in the sack. He strode over to assess the situation.

As he drew closer, Gideon realized he could see the light through the windows more clearly than usual. He opened the door and groaned. Miriam sat on a bench, her elbows propped on the table, her face buried in a pot holder, of all things. Her shoulders shuddered with her nearly silent weeping.

He went and sat beside her, his back against the table and his hip alongside her skirts. As soon as he reached for her, she tumbled sideways into his chest. She cried brokenheartedly— just the way Mama had when Pa died. Gideon remembered it well. He felt just as helpless as he had then. Wrapping his arms securely about Miriam and holding fast was all he could do—precious little to guard her tender heart from such terrible news.

When she finally wound down, he gave her time to let his presence sink in. Hopefully she'd find consolation in knowing she'd not be left alone in her first moments of grief. She mopped her tear-ravaged face with the pot holder, and he tenderly stroked her brow. "You're tuckered out. I want you to sleep the whole day away. We'll talk things over this evening."

He stood and thought about letting her walk back into the bedroom. Her movements as she stood and stepped around the edge of the bench were stilted, and her features looked bleakly wooden. If her appearance alone wasn't reason enough, the obstacles in her path convinced him she'd never make it. Gideon swept her into his arms. She sagged against him and whispered in a shaky voice, "What about Hannah's babies?"

"They're right as rain. God never made cuter dumplin's. You'll meet them after you've rested up. Young as they are, they'll run you ragged if you don't store up a bit of energy."

As he spoke, he plowed through everything cluttering the floor and into the room where his brothers all sat, fully dressed and waiting for a chance to escape from a woman's weeping. He didn't bother to introduce them. He simply passed by all of them and tucked her into his bed while they hastily exited the room.

He suffered an awkward moment, realizing she'd not want to shed her robe in his presence. She'd fallen fast asleep earlier; she probably didn't comprehend he'd already seen her in her bedgown.

Miriam shivered.

Relief flooded him. He considered the room much too warm from having his brothers sleeping in it all night. Obviously Miriam thought otherwise. "That one blanket won't be enough to keep you warm, Miss Miriam. You'd best keep on your robe for a bit of extra bundling." He settled her onto his mattress. The mattress smelled a mite stale. How long had it been since he replaced the cornhusks and hay inside the ticking? He couldn't rightly remember. No use fretting over anything that minor. He pulled up the cover and tucked it around her narrow shoulders. "Sweet dreams."

"I apologize for being such a bother."

"You're not a bother. Now hush and sleep." He turned, paced out of the room, and shut the door to give her privacy.

All five men sat at the breakfast table, drank Miriam's restaurant-perfect coffee, and ate her melt-in-your-mouth biscuits. Titus looked around. "This place is a pigsty."

Gideon nodded. "I don't want her waking up and coming out to this. Hannah was always finicky about cleanliness; I don't imagine Miss Miriam will be any less so. Bryce, you get all of the stuff up off the floor and carry it back out to the stable. Titus, you wash the dishes. I don't reckon we have a clean one left in the whole house."

Gideon knew his brothers didn't welcome those orders. Because they all worked from can-see-to-can't, seven days a week, those chores normally went undone. They'd shed the burden of domestic frills as soon as there wasn't a woman around to protest. The problem was, a woman occupied the house again.

He continued, "Logan, you're going to have to use sand to scrub the junk off the floor. Everyone needs to get back in the habit of scraping off their boots before they come in. For a few days here, we're gonna have to act civilized."

Bryce scowled at him. "You're mighty good at makin' us do the dirty work. What're you putting your hand to?"

Gideon wrinkled his nose. "I'm going to wash the stuff from her clothes."

Logan nodded. "I got it on mine, too. I'll toss them in the pot."

Gideon muttered as all of them volunteered him to do their

laundry. He'd rather do just about anything but laundry. Since he was the eldest, he usually managed to order someone else to do the chore. The only reason he'd been ready to do it was because he didn't cotton to the notion of his brothers touching prim little Miriam's unmentionables. Frankly, he didn't want to deal with them, either. It went against all decency, but he'd left her trunks in town, and the woman needed something to wear. *Stuck between a rattler and a brushfire.* Gideon let out a gusty sigh. "Let's get to work."

Everyone set to his chores. Titus left most of the dishes to soak in three big tubs. He took the pots down to the creek for a sand scouring. Bryce hauled an armful of junk out to the stable, then milked the cow before he came back. He set down the milk pail, hauled out the harness, and came back with the eggs he'd gathered.

Logan took out the swill to slop the hogs, came back, scowled at the floor, and grumbled, "Don't know why I have to scrub it. It'll be dirty again, soon as anyone walks across it. Can't see wasting my time." His brothers all gave him nasty looks, so he grabbed the broom.

After shaving half a cake of soap into the wash kettle, Gideon set it over a fire in the yard and filled it with water. As it started to heat, he paced back into the cabin. Quietly as he could, he eased the bedroom door open and tiptoed in. He stood still for a moment, but he didn't hear a thing. Every step he took sounded clumsily loud as he walked across the planks to gather shirts and britches off the pegs and floor. Finally, he reached the far side of the room and paused outside the blanket partition.

"Miss Miriam, I aim to fetch the laundry if you don't mind."

She failed to answer, so he peered in to be sure she was

okay. He strained to listen and heard soft breaths in a slow, deep cadence. *Good. She's sleeping.* Moving away, he snagged his shirts off the pegs, used the toe of his boot to hook out the blanket stacked with her soiled clothing, and finally went to the other end. He reached under the bed to get his grime-encrusted britches.

In morning light, she looked more delicate, more ethereal. The way her braid unraveled across the pillow invited a man to test each rippling, golden wave.

Hannah's kid sister—the one he'd heard her mention and somehow pictured as a schoolgirl in pigtails—was an eyeful of femininity. Gideon tamped down that line of thought and beat a hasty retreat. He left the clothes by the boiling laundry pot and headed toward Daniel's tiny cottage.

The Chance men never stood on formalities. Gideon walked in without knocking and scooped Polly from the floor. Over at the table, Daniel tried to get Virginia to take one more sip of apple cider. The two of them seemed to be wearing more of the contents of the glass than drinking it.

"I'm doing laundry," Gideon announced as he started to toss clothes into a crate.

"Great!"

After he filled the crate, he turned and looked at his brother. Daniel showed remarkable patience with his two little ones. Three-year-old Polly chattered twenty to the dozen, and Virginia had hit the walking stage a few days earlier.

Once Hannah died, Daniel had advertised for a housekeeper, but the only one who responded made it clear she held far more interest in matrimony than in mending. After a short time, it became clear that for the sake of Daniel's sanity, the Chance brothers were going to have to handle matters on their own. They devised a simple solution: Each man took a day every week to watch the girls. Daniel took both Wednesday and Sunday since the girls were his, and he minded them from sundown to sunup all of the time.

"Dan, we've got a visitor."

"Oh?" Daniel wiped Ginny Mae's face. "Who?"

Gideon watched his brother intently. "Miriam Hancock came into town last night."

"Miriam?" Dan looked dazed. "What is she doing here?"

"It seems Hannah wrote her and mentioned she didn't feel well. Miriam came to help her out."

"Why'd she do a foolish thing like that? Letters take up to eight months to get there!"

"Don't ask me to figure out the mind of a woman. Fact remains, Miriam is here. I figured I'd best tell you before you ran into her in the yard. I'm sure she'll want to see her nieces today."

"How long is she planning to stay?"

"I didn't ask."

As it was Saturday, it was Gideon's day to have the girls. He popped both of them into the fenced-off play area Daniel had made to contain the girls while his brothers did yard chores. Some of the clothes were so badly soiled, Gideon couldn't even put them in the wash kettle. He toted them down to the creek, knelt, and swished the worst of the grime from them. Beating them on a rock worked, but he had neither the time nor patience to do much of that. Instead, he hauled them all back to the fire.

Steam rose from the huge, cast-iron cauldron. The soap bubbled a bit on the surface. Yeah, that looked just like it did when Mama used to have laundry day. Satisfied with the wash water, he dumped in Miriam's white clothes and stirred them with a paddle. After he made sure they'd come clean, he double rinsed them so the lye residue wouldn't irritate her delicate skin or rot the thin cotton fabric, then wrung out each snowy garment and hung it on the clothesline. It seemed mighty strange to see a woman's things there.

He washed the baby's white things next, then did the rest of the laundry. It was a hot, miserable job, and he didn't feel guilty in the least for how he kept leaving things in the pot to boil a bit while he went off to tickle Polly or play peekaboo with Ginny Mae.

Once all the clothes fluttered in the wind, he hitched each of the girls under his arms and hiked over to the garden. They played in the dirt and mud while he staked up the tomatoes and watered the melons and beans. Polly was giggling, and Ginny Mae just about put a worm in her mouth when Gideon looked up to see Miriam standing there. He snatched the worm from Ginny Mae and stammered, "They're dirty right now, but they're good girls."

A tender smile lit her face. "They're beautiful, and they'll clean up. Little girls deserve to make mud pies." She self-consciously tugged at her robe, then stooped down. Instead of grabbing, she simply opened her arms. Polly went right to her. "Hello, poppet. You're my Polly-girl, and you are every bit as precious as your mama said."

Polly rubbed her hand up and down the soft fabric of her aunt's green dressing gown. "Pretty."

A becoming blush stained her cheeks. "Yes, well, Auntie Miriam needs her clothes."

"They're on the clothesline. It's hot today, so they'll be dry in a few hours," Gideon said.

"What about my trunks?"

"They're in town. I'll see if we can't fetch them in a day or two."

"In the meantime, I'll take the girls inside with me. There's plenty to do. I'm sure you have more than enough to accomplish."

He looked at her, then slowly said, "It's my day to have the girls."

"Your day?"

"We each take a day. Daniel takes two days since they're his daughters."

Still fussing with her dressing gown, she murmured, "Seeing as I'm able to mind the girls, I'm sure you have much to do elsewhere."

"I won't deny that, but I don't know that leaving the girls with you is such a keen plan. Polly doesn't cotton to strangers."

"Polly and I will get along famously." One of the brothers walked past. Miriam wasn't sure which one he was, but she blushed at the way he eyed her in her nightwear. "So if you'll excuse us, we'll be off."

He cast a glance at his brother's back, then eyed her attire with a frown. "You can't traipse around in that all day. Borrow something from your sister's trunk."

"I don't know if I can. I—"

"I'll handle it with Daniel. Go on inside."

She took both girls back toward the cottage. The dirt felt good under her bare feet. After all of that time on a ship, she wanted solid earth beneath her for the rest of her days. The slight breeze carried the scents of pine, horses, and hay. Men's baritones mingled in the background, a deep counterpoint to the musical trills of songbirds and scolds of jays.

This place was all that her life in the islands had not been. The air felt dry, not humid. The flowers were plentiful but tiny instead of cloying and exuberant. Browns and muted greens dominated the landscape instead of a kaleidoscope of brilliant jewel tones. These men crowded in one home, shared one bedroom. This was a far cry from the stringent rules they lived by back home to ensure privacy, modesty, and decorum. In odd juxtaposition to that, everyone here—except for her, she thought wryly—was completely dressed; whereas back home, the natives wore only the barest minimum.

Dear, sweet Hannah scribbled letters in secret, telling how she hated living here. Homesickness, she confessed, plagued her. The cold weather made her spirits plummet, and no matter how hard she worked, everything looked dismal and dusty. The brothers were all good men, but she felt sadly outnumbered and lonely for female companionship. Mama and Daddy listened to Miriam's offer to go help her sister with grave misgivings, but they'd decided it was for the best. Clearly, with six men and a second child on the way, Hannah couldn't take care of matters on her own anymore.

As Miriam left, Mama had whispered, "There are no decent, God-fearing white men here for you, darling. Surely Miriam will introduce you to a few worthy young men of good character."

Miriam looked about and cuddled the girls a bit closer. Worthy young men wouldn't be a part of her life. Moping about that wouldn't do much good. All her life, Papa taught her to deal with whatever God allowed to happen in life without complaint. Hannah heard that same speech countless times, so for her to have poured out her laments underscored the gravity of her plight.

Miriam ached to have a husband and children of her own. At twenty, she didn't exactly rate as an old maid, but she couldn't expect Daniel and his brothers to play matchmaker for her. Since she'd come and Hannah was gone, she knew her destiny lay in being a spinster aunt. Surely God sent her here. These girls needed a woman's caring. Polly's tangled and matted hair bore mute testimony to that fact. Miriam quietly and immediately accepted the bittersweet fact that if she couldn't have a man and babes of her own, she'd at least have dear Hannah's wee ones to cherish.

Off to the side of the main house, two big trees bracketed a tiny cottage. Hannah's letters mentioned the brothers building a "habitation" for her. Surely this was it. Miriam hitched Virginia Mae higher on her hip and stepped across the threshold. The building was a tiny box of a place—a simple, one-room affair. Once she winced at the mess, Miriam noted the room featured no kitchen. The fireplace was tiny—only enough to warm this little place but not big enough to cook over. A small cabinet on the wall and a pint-sized table and chairs were the only things that defined one corner. The rest of the place held a bed, a trundle that was undoubtedly Polly's, and a crib for the baby. She deduced Hannah must've been making meals for all six of the Chance men over at the main house.

Unable to navigate the room without stepping and tripping on things, Miriam made a game of picking up Daniel's possessions. The little toddlers had fun holding items up for her reactions. She'd pinch her nose and point at one corner for laundry. Though someone had done laundry today, they'd missed half of the load from this residence.

It was more than embarrassing to stay in her nightwear. She checked the clothesline and sighed. Her sodden clothes still dripped on the line. Unaccustomed to the weather here, she couldn't tell how long before her dress would be dry. Much as she didn't want to go through Hannah's things, Miriam decided to obey Gideon's instructions.

Back in the cottage, she found Hannah's trunk. As she opened the lid, Miriam cried. They'd always shared clothes, and she knew her sister wouldn't begrudge her these essentials; but the scent of Hannah's perfume brought back a flood of memories, and seeing her favorite fan, even touching her clothing, tore at Miriam. She desperately wanted to slam the lid back down. Gideon said they'd fetch her things in a few days—surely she could tolerate wearing only one set of clothing for a while.

Ginny Mae tugged on her arm. The sleeve pulled, causing the wrapped bodice of her robe to gap and expose her nightgown. Miriam pulled the baby into her lap and cradled her there. Polly tugged on the other side.

"I gotta go potty, Auntie Miri-Em."

Miriam hadn't located a chamber pot in this mess. She dried her tears. "Can you wait just a minute, Polly?"

Polly nodded.

Miriam hastily went through the trunk. The pieced skirt on the blue dress didn't conform to any style. *Feed sacks. Hannah made these out of feed sacks—and she stitched huge waists to permit her room for her family condition.* Miriam delved deeper and located a rose-colored gown she'd sewn for her sister's trousseau. That and a few other essentials would serve satisfactorily. She latched the cottage door shut and changed.

Once she'd dressed, Miriam took Polly to the outhouse and came back to the little cottage. Dressed in decent attire, she felt free to move about and do whatever she deemed fit. She opened the door wide to air out the cottage and dusted. Polly followed her like a lonely little puppy, and Virginia Mae toddled behind. Miriam gave them each a cloth, and they "helped." She shoved the trundle beneath the bed, then picked up a few more stray items that had fallen there before she swept.

Spoons and cups went onto the table, and blankets were piled onto the beds. Whimsical wooden animals kept turning up. The Chance men must enjoy whittling, because they'd turned out a plethora of miniature beasts. Miriam admired each one for her little nieces, then stored them all in a bowl. "Like Noah's ark," she said.

Polly gave her a perplexed look.

Miriam knelt and used the bowl like a boat as she tried to remind the little tyke about the Bible story. Clearly Polly hadn't heard it before. That fact alarmed Miriam. Weren't these men rearing the girls to know the holy scriptures?

Miriam busied the girls with the wooden creatures and set to earnest work. The clothesline had a bit more space on it, but she earmarked that for the remaining laundry. The blankets all needed airing, so she cast them over several shrubs and weighted them down with a few rocks to keep them from blowing into the dirt. Though it seemed bold, she stripped the sheets from Daniel's bed and added them to the laundry pile. Her nose wrinkled in distaste. Now that she thought about it, there hadn't been a single sheet on any of the beds back in the main house. These men were barely civilized.

Boots crunched leaves outside. Miriam turned as Gideon filled the doorway and cast a shadow across the room.

"This place hasn't looked like this since—" He stopped short, then finished diplomatically, "For a long time."

They exchanged stricken looks, then Miriam pivoted to the side and washed her hands in a bucket. She dipped in a cloth and swiped at the dust and mud on Virginia's hands and face. "I assume it's close to your luncheon hour. The girls and I will come to the big house and—"

She didn't finish. Someone else arrived. Miriam heard a shocked gasp. Though she hadn't heard it in almost five years, she recognized Daniel's voice. "Hannah!"

five

Gideon watched Miriam go stark still. She slowly turned, and deep sadness painted her features. Tears glistened in her eyes. "Daniel. I'm so sorry—"

Sensing his brother's shock, Gideon braced his arm. This was a terrible blow. Daniel had adored his bride, and the grief still ate at him. The longing and hope on his face changed to nothing short of hatred.

"Dan, I told her to—"

"How dare you! Take that off."

Miriam's lips parted in shock.

Daniel leaned forward, and his hands knotted to fists that shook with the effort it took to keep them down at his sides. He demanded in a tone that trembled with rage, "Take it off! How dare you touch her things!"

"Dan—" Gideon tried to calm his brother but to no avail.

Daniel shook off Gideon's hand, wheeled around, and plowed out the door. Virginia Mae's voice echoed in the suddenly all-too-quiet cottage. "Daddy! Daddy!"

Gideon turned back to Miriam. She'd curled her hands around the slats of a chair as if to shore herself up after receiving a hefty blow. She kept blinking and breathed through her mouth to hold back the tears that welled up. "Miriam, I'm sorry. This was my fault."

She bit her lip, then quavered, "Please go give him my apology."

His heart went out to her. She'd just followed his instructions and hadn't knowingly done anything to upset her brother-in-law. Truth be told, she did look enough like her sister to cause a grieving man to mistake her for the woman he'd loved. He searched to find the right words to soften her hurt, but nothing came to mind.

"Please," she whispered brokenly, "go."

Gideon nodded once, then left her to whatever anguish she felt. Of all his brothers, Daniel was the most volatile. Five years ago, he'd been off drinking in San Francisco when he got shanghaied. While his ship docked in the islands, he'd met Hannah. He never said a thing about that year of his life. He'd come back a more contained, disciplined man. Gideon wasn't sure whether marriage or his time aboard ship had done that, but since Hannah died, there were days when Daniel's rage knew no bounds.

Daniel went out to the woodpile. The ring of the ax splitting wood let Gideon know where he was and to keep a wary distance. He stood and watched his brother work himself into a full lather before he finally said, "It was a shock, Dan, but she didn't mean to upset you. It's my fault—I told her to borrow something."

Daniel set the next piece on the chopping stump and split it with a single, powerful blow. The storm in his eyes matched the violence of his action. He set the next log up, then gritted, "No one touches my Hannah's things. No one."

"Fair enough."

"Get rid of that woman. I don't want her here."

It was worse than he'd imagined. Gideon hitched his hip and half-sat on the fence. He moved slowly in an effort to appear casual and untroubled. "I don't reckon that's going to be possible for a few days. She came a long ways and needs to rest before—"

Daniel cut him off by repeating in an unyielding tone, "I don't want her here."

"What did she ever do to you?"

"Look at her. Just look! They could have been twins!"

The anguish behind Daniel's words let Gideon know his brother's shock was still too fresh and raw. "All right, Dan. I understand. We'll get rid of her as soon as possible." He paused, then added, "In the meantime, you're going to have to be civil to her."

"That's not a problem. I'm not going to see her."

Gideon's patience started to unravel. He'd managed precious little sleep last night and wasn't of a mind to put up with a brother having a tantrum. He fought to keep an even tone. "You're a better man than that, Dan."

Daniel hefted the ax. His knuckles were white as he gripped the handle, raised the blade, and buried it into the stump. He stared at the deeply marred place he'd wedged the blade and didn't look up as he said in a mere rasp, "You don't know what you're asking."

"Maybe not—but if you had any notion how brave that little gal tried to be after you thundered at her and left, you'd try to match her courage." He figured he'd said as much as he dared. Gideon straightened up. "We'll see you for dinner."

"Supper."

He let out a snort and walked off. Half an hour later, Gideon walked into the house. It looked miles better after all of his brothers had tended to their assigned chores. They'd all need to hustle a fair bit to get the real work done, but from the smell of things, Miriam's cooking would be ample reward for their efforts.

Miriam. Dressed in the gown he'd just washed for her, she stood over by the stove. Though not exactly wet, the garment rated as excessively damp. She made no reference to that point, even though it had to feel clammy. He hoped she wouldn't catch a chill from wearing it. Overall, the dress didn't exactly cling to her, but a man would have to be dead and buried not to notice the way every last inch of the cloth accentuated a very feminine shape. Miriam seemingly ignored her uncomfortable clothing and diligently worked over a few pots.

She lifted a lid on something, and Gideon's mouth watered. One of his brothers didn't even bother to muffle his groan. When she started to dish servings onto a plate, Gideon stated, "Don't make so much work for yourself, Miss Miriam. Just stick the pots on the table. We'll serve ourselves."

She set aside that plate. Without a word, she did as he bade. His other brothers filed in and sniffed the air appreciably. "Whatever you whipped up, it sure does make a feller's nose take notice," Bryce said.

Miriam shot him a wobbly smile. Gideon sat and swept Polly into his lap. "Bet you're a hungry little bear today."

"Uh-huh. She maded 'tatoes."

Logan chuckled. "Now you've done it, Miss Miriam. You made a friend for life. Polly loves taters."

All of the men sat and started to fill their plates. Miriam stayed at the stove and cut the food on the plate she'd already dished up. One place at the table remained conspicuously vacant. Titus said in a slightly too jovial tone, "Come sit here with us, Miss Miriam."

Gideon's fork was halfway to Polly's mouth when Miriam shook her head. Polly grabbed for the bite. Miriam poured a bit of gravy on her plate, then set the gravy boat in the center of the table. She gently swept Virginia Mae from Bryce's hold and claimed the plate from the stove.

"Aw, I can feed her. We're all pretty fair hands at that kind of stuff," Bryce said.

"I'm sure you are." Miriam's gaze swept across the already decimated pots, bowls, and half-cleared plates. Her features went taut. A soundless sigh heaved her bosom, and she left. Gideon scowled. "Hey. Come back here."

Her voice drifted over her shoulder, "Ginny Mae's wet."

In no time at all, the brothers finished off every last speck of food. Daniel hadn't gotten to eat, but if he didn't bother to show up, he had no call to bellyache. Food this good deserved to be appreciated down to the last bite. They'd eaten real loaf bread for the first time in ages. Normally they ate either sticky or rock-hard biscuits. She must have kneaded the loaves before she came out to the garden.

"She set beans to soak," Bryce reported. "Think she'll sweeten them and add in ham or bacon?"

"I reckon whatever she does," Titus said as he sopped up the gravy with the last crust of his bread, "it'll be better than anything we've had in a coon's age."

Logan sighed appreciatively. "She sure can cook."

"Yeah, well, quit mooning over the vittles and get back to work. Logan, you take the buckboard to town and fetch Miss Miriam's trunks. If I so much as catch a whiff of beer or whiskey on you when you get home, I'll tan your hide so you can't sit 'til Christmas."

Titus pumped a bucket of water and dumped the plates into it. He took Polly and said, "I reckon it's best we keep the girls to their naps. I'll go tuck this little one in and bring back Miss Miriam's plate."

By the time Titus returned, Paul, Logan, and Bryce were long gone. Gideon moved the bucket with the trout onto the table and hoped Miriam would pan-fry them for supper. He had a hankering for a nicely turned hunk of trout. Titus interrupted his longings. "She fed Ginny and was singing her off to sleep."

"How did Polly do?"

"Much as she don't cotton to strangers, she truly does head straight to Miss Miriam for a pat or a smile. I told her they both nap a good while this time of the day."

"I hope she naps, too."

"I don't much think so. She asked me where Hannah's grave was."

Gideon grimaced.

"I think you'd best leave her alone. She didn't look none too good. Kind of reminded me of the air Mama carried when she needed us to leave her be."

"I'd better go, anyway. Daniel might be there."

"Nah. I just saw him. He's taking all the logs he split to the woodpile."

Supper came, and Gideon tried not to make a spectacle of himself when Miriam set a platter of trout on the table. Every last piece was fried to crispy, golden brown perfection. She served rice and greens, too. Her day gown was dry. Polly kept a fistful of it and shadowed her every move.

"Logan, go on over to the cottage and bring back a chair," Gideon ordered under his breath. "Put it at the foot of the table so Miriam has a place."

Paul brought in the evening milking and asked, "Where do you want this, Miss Miriam?"

"What is it?"

"Milk. I already strained it for you."

"Do you men drink it or do just the girls?"

"Depends on whether you need any milk for your cooking."

"Why don't you save half of it," she said uncertainly, then turned to open the oven door. Gideon's mouth watered. The fragrance had teased him ever since he came inside, but he'd tried to deny the possibility. Cobbler. He inhaled deeply. Apple.

"Lord, have mercy," Bryce moaned.

Miriam set the cobbler on the stove top and shut the door. She moved stiffly and said with great precision, "I hope that was a prayer, because I will not have the Lord's name taken in vain."

"Sorry, ma'am. I mean, miss. You surely can take that as a prayer of thanksgiving."

Logan arrived with the chair. With supper on the table, everyone flocked to the benches. Gideon seated Miriam and tried to take Polly back with him, but she wouldn't turn loose of her aunt. "Here, poppet." Miriam gently lifted their niece onto her lap. She wrapped her arms around Polly's and folded their hands together into a steeple. "Who asks the blessing?"

The chorus of uncomfortable "uhs" left Gideon embarrassed. He took his seat as Daniel came in. Daniel answered with undisguised hostility, "Nobody prays here."

"Papa always said things can change," Miriam said. She kept hold of Polly's little hands, dipped her head, and whispered, "I'll say something, then you say it, too."

Polly nodded.

"Dear God," Miriam began.

"Dear God—"

"We give Thee thanks for our food."

"Thee thanks for food."

A few more quick lines, and they finished off with a duet of "Amen."

The whole while, the other brothers respectfully bowed their heads; but Dan had made a point of reaching across the table, noisily serving himself, and grunting a disdainful snort. Gideon resolved to string him up by his heels if he tried that stunt again.

As they filled their plates, Logan said, "Mama taught us a different grace."

"Then you may teach it to us tomorrow," Miriam said as she tied a dishcloth around Polly's neck.

Polly chattered and Daniel's brothers tried to make conversation to cover his stony silence. Miriam spoke when directly addressed but otherwise stayed quiet. Her responses were softly spoken and brief, as if she was doing her best to be polite and invisible at the same time. He caught the way she hesitantly glanced at Dan out of the corner of her eye and winced at how her shoulders curled forward just the tiniest bit. Gideon noticed how Miriam's hands shook and worried over her pallor. He'd talk to her after supper and promise that, mad as Daniel might be, she had no cause to fear he'd ever raise a hand to her.

Bowls got passed around again, and his brothers scraped every last morsel of food out of the pans and onto their plates. Gideon thought to offer her more, but she didn't eat much of what was on her plate, so it seemed silly to ask if she wanted anything else. More went into Polly's mouth than her own.

The tension bugged him. He said nothing because Miriam and Daniel would have to work things out between themselves. Surely by morning, Dan would come to terms with the situation and could be counted on to behave himself decently for a few days 'til Miriam went back home.

Once supper was over, Dan swiped little Polly straight off of Miriam's lap without so much as a word of warning. Only the ring of his boots on the floor planks broke the crackling silence until he reached the door. He kicked the door shut behind himself.

Every last brother watched as Miriam flinched. Bryce opened his mouth, but Gideon booted him under the table to keep him from saying something stupid.

Titus offered, "I'll wash the dishes. Paul, you dry."

"Fine." Gideon stood. "Bryce, see to the beasts and be sure to check that latch on the chicken coop."

Miriam wet her lips, then murmured, "Please excuse me." She slipped out of her chair and across the floor, her gait a soundless glide. Then she shut the door behind herself noiselessly.

"Poor thing," Titus mumbled.

"Sadder'n a hound that tangled with a porkypine," Bryce added.

Paul smacked the tabletop, and all of the dishes jumped. "Dan tries that again, and I'm gonna deck him!"

Though he privately agreed, Gideon didn't want his brothers brawling. "No one's going to do anything." He glared at his brothers. "All you'll do is pour kerosene on his temper if you stand up for her. His temper will burn hotter, and she'll get the blast. Stay out of it."

"Now wait just a minute—"

"No, you all hold your horses." Gideon folded his arms across his chest and stared them down. "Some things are best left alone. Dan's raging, but he'll run out of steam. In the meantime, just try to keep her away from him. He'll come to his senses."

"It ain't a matter of keeping her away from him," Bryce groused. "It's a matter of keeping him away from her."

"No," Gideon said heavily. "He can't bear the sight of her. She looks too much like Hannah."

"Ain't her fault, Giddy." Bryce cocked his head to the side and continued as if he'd come to a brilliant deduction. "They were sisters."

Titus ignored Bryce and stacked dishes into a bucket. "The real problem is going to be keeping her away from the kids."

"I don't give a hang if Dan doesn't want her seeing them,"

Gideon decided. "There's nothing wrong with her singing and playing with them."

"More likely *praying*," Logan corrected him.

"Yeah," Gideon stared back, "but Hannah and Mama both would've done the selfsame things. Until she leaves, let her enjoy them. We've jawed about this enough. You all pitch in and get things done."

Gideon fought the urge to dab his thumb into a little pile of sugar and cinnamon crumbs left from the cobbler. He'd love that last little taste, but he needed to look stern and in control just now. Sucking a sweet off of his thumb would spoil the effect. Instead, he picked up his plate and shoved it on the top of the teetering stack in Titus's bucket.

A few more minutes passed. Gideon figured Miriam had gone off to the privy and taken a little extra time to regain her composure, but when she didn't come back after a while, he grew concerned. He didn't want his brothers setting off like hounds after a frightened hare, so he silently went in search.

The privy was empty, the door hanging off to the side in careless disregard to privacy. They'd left it that way so Polly wouldn't be afraid of the dark when they took her there. With Miriam visiting, that needed to be fixed—at least temporarily. All day long, little details like that illustrated just how lackadaisical they'd become in regard to propriety. Having a woman around—even for a handful of days—was making his to-do list grow by leaps and bounds.

Gideon pondered where to turn next. Since his brother had told him she'd asked about the grave, he paced toward the tall pines. Wildflowers lay at the base of the wooden marker Daniel had carved as Hannah's headstone. That had to be Miriam's doing, because Dan hadn't ever once taken flowers to it.

Where was Miriam?

six

He found her in the garden. A small basket with a trio of tomatoes and a pair of small melons lay in the soil by her skirts. At first, Gideon thought Miriam was on her knees, leaning forward to pick something. It took a second for him to realize she'd doubled over. She'd huddled down like a pitifully cold little rabbit that couldn't find its way back to the warren. The backs of her hands rested in the loam, and her fingers curled upward to cup her forehead. She looked so vulnerable and forlorn. He hunkered down beside her and tried to take stock of the situation.

Placing a tentative hand on her shoulder, he murmured, "Miss Miriam? You all right?"

"Head hurts," she whispered in a voice thick with tears.

"Aw, sweet pea, I'll bet it does." He eased his weight onto his knees and pulled her into his arms. She came unresistingly, but she didn't nestle into him for comfort, either. She was too limp to do anything.

Gideon called himself ten kinds of a fool. After the way Logan flattened her and knocked her noggin, she still had to be feeling poorly. Gideon carefully cupped her head to his chest and amended his assessment. The lump beneath his fingers made him wonder why she hadn't been cross-eyed and sick as a hound dog. Why had he let her cook and clean most of the day when he'd originally told her to sleep? He should have hauled her back to the house and tied her to the bed instead of letting her wear herself to a frazzle.

Just as bad, she still needed time after getting the awful news. One good cry didn't wash away grief. It was a marvel she hadn't dissolved into a puddle of tears over the way Daniel treated her.

Gideon's fingers slid beneath her thick golden braid and slowly kneaded her nape. Her breath hitched. Every last inch of her shuddered. "Aww," he murmured, unable to concoct anything meaningful for such a catastrophic time. Her breath hitched again, and he snuggled her closer. He'd tried hard to be strong after Pa and Mama each died, but he'd ridden Splotch off to a secluded spot and shed his fair share of bitter, aching tears, too. Folks expected a man to be strong, even in adversity, but a woman. . .

Well, a woman wasn't supposed to be this brave. She'd spent the last scraps of her composure when Daniel thundered at her, then later at supper. Clearly she was spoiling for a decent caterwaul. "Might as well let loose," he whispered into her soft hair.

"Weeping w—won't make it an—nee bet—ter," she whispered in choppy syllables that made her frame bump against him.

"Holding it all in won't lessen it," he countered. His words freed her, at least to some degree. Tears silently slipped down her cheeks and wet his shirt. He could almost taste the salt in them.

Crickets chirped and cicadas whirred. Horses whinnied and the cow lowed. One of the dogs barked a few times. Gideon knelt there and wished he were anywhere else. He wasn't cut out to comfort a grieving woman. He felt awkward and stupid. Had he thought even once, poor little Miriam wouldn't have worked herself into such a frazzled mess.

Right now the bitty, worn-out woman needed rest more than anything. His bed would have to do. It didn't quite seem fitting for her to be sleeping in a room with a bunch of men. Even Mama hadn't when they moved here.

A banker had cheated them out of their old ranch when Pa died. They'd packed up everything they owned and pretty much started fresh here. Mama was always first up and last to bed, so she'd slept in a bedstead in the main room. Since the stove sat a stone's throw away from her mattress, she'd been warm enough during the coldest winter nights.

That bed now filled a fair part of the floor space in Daniel's cabin. If Miriam were feeling any better, she ought to sleep in the cabin with the girls and have Daniel share the main house with his brothers. That wouldn't be wise tonight. She wasn't feeling up to tending the girls if they woke, and asking Daniel to give up his home and let Miriam sleep in Hannah's bed would likely set off his temper. No, tonight Miriam would have to sleep where she'd spent the previous night.

Gideon slowly rose and planned to carry her in, but she gained her feet and wrapped her arms about herself. He wondered whether she did it because she was cold, or if it was a subconscious way of comforting herself or guarding against the oppressive grief. Either way, he drew her into the lee of his body.

She fit there all too easily and molded her frame to his, making him aware again how fragile and soft women were. Somehow it felt good and right to have her in his arms, but just as quickly as that notion sneaked through his mind, he rejected it.

Bad enough they'd buried Mama and Hannah beneath the majestic pines over to the east of the house. Miriam was every bit as small as her sister had been. Two graves seemed like more than one ranch's fair share for such a short span of time. Sure as shootin', if Miriam stayed more than just a few days, she'd end up raising the count to three. This was no land for a delicate woman. Gideon resolved to hustle her out of here right quick.

"I'm s—sorry."

Her apology jarred him out of his grim decision making. "No, sweet pea. You've no call to beg my pardon," he said quietly. He hoped if he kept his tone low, he'd spare her a bit of throbbing in her head. "You have a tender heart is all." *That, and a body that's as vulnerable as your spirit.* "Let's tuck you in for the night."

He shortened his stride and led her back to the house. Only Paul was inside. He sat by the hearth, sharpening knives on a whetstone. He looked up, and his lips thinned as he took in Miriam's red eyes and nose. Gideon shook his head in a silent warning. Miriam didn't need anyone commenting on the obvious.

She eased away from his side and went to the washstand. For an instant, Gideon worried the pitcher would be empty as usual; but she lifted it, and fresh water trickled into the chipped porcelain basin. Of course. Of course Miss Miriam would have refilled it.

An odd impression struck him. She wasn't prissy about being tidy the way Hannah had been. The corners of Hannah's mouth seemed perpetually tightened, as if she disapproved of just about everything. Oh, she'd pitched in and done all the woman-work. She'd been sweet as honey to Daniel, too. No one would ever fault her on how loving she'd been to little Polly.

More than anything, Gideon came away with the feeling his brother's wife felt a tad put out with the fact of having more than just her own man to care for. He wasn't the only one who sensed her resentment, either. His brothers all yielded to Hannah's picky little preferences and allowed her some of her weepy days. After all, she'd been in a delicate condition nearly two of the three years she'd lived with them.

Then, too, a woman had a right to want a nest of her own. When Daniel appeared out of the blue with a wife, the brothers jumped in and built the cottage straightaway. Though Hannah and Daniel slept there, the fireplace was only sufficient for heat. During the winter, Hannah needed to do the laundry here in the big house, and she'd done the cooking here year 'round. Mama always said cooking for two or ten didn't make much difference, but Gideon suspected Hannah would have disagreed.

So far, Miss Miriam didn't seem to mind stepping in front of a stove. Then again, it wasn't a permanent arrangement. She'd only be here a few brief days, so making fancy meals with all the fixin's probably suited her. After being stuck on the sailing ship, having the freedom to decide what to eat might well be a treat to her.

Nonetheless, the first thing she'd done was set to sprucing up the place that first night. In his experience, when grief struck, folks did one of two things: They either took to their beds or lost themselves in their usual tasks. Resorting to habits and tasks helped them numb some of the impact of the sorrow. For her to have put her hand to such labor hinted that she was in the habit of keeping a tidy home. Orderliness seemed to be something that came deep from within—not the result of a rule she followed for the sake of being virtuous.

Watching her wash up felt wrong, so he turned away. When the soft splashing stopped, Gideon saw the frown on Paul's face and turned to see the cause. Miriam had folded her handkerchief, dampened it, and pressed the compress to her forehead as she braced herself against the washstand with the other hand. Her chin rested on her chest as if her head had grown too heavy to hold up.

Gideon closed the distance between them in a heartbeat. "Miss Miriam?"

She turned toward him, and he slipped his arms around her. Poor little gal had run out of steam. Even then, she didn't slump against him. Her hanky got his shirt damp as she whispered, "I know it's a bit early yet, but would you mind too awfully much if I lie down?"

"It would bother me if you didn't." He stooped a bit, hooked an arm behind her knees, and lifted. Once he carried her behind the blanket-curtain in the back room, he set Miriam down and nudged her to sit on his bed. Taking pains to keep his voice low, he ordered, "You go on and get ready for bed. I'll see if I can rustle up some willow bark for your headache."

"That's very kind of you to offer," she half whispered. "Truly, I believe sleep is all I need."

Later he went to peek in on her. She'd huddled into a ball and fallen asleep—but that knowledge brought him no relief because the pillow and her cheeks were wet with more tears.

Being a man of the cloth, her father would have known the right things to say. Miriam needed flowery words of eternal peace and assurance. Gideon knew none of them. At the ripe old age of twenty-six, he reckoned he was far too old to learn them now.

In the morning, he'd check on how she felt and make plans to send her back home. To be sure, she'd need two, maybe even three days before he put her aboard a ship. It would let her come to grips with the fact that Hannah had passed on to the hereafter and also give Miriam a chance to play a bit with Polly and Ginny Mae. That way, she'd go back home with a few sweet memories to soften the blow.

He'd ask to see her ticket and make inquiries as to when that company had the next ship slated for departure. The ranch needed supplies. He'd take her back to the docks, and soon as her ship set sail, he'd fill up the buckboard and bring back essentials. That way, he'd only miss one day's work instead of two.

Gideon came back out and took out a sheet of paper. He whittled the nib of his pen and set the inkwell on the clean tabletop. It was nice, sitting down to a clear writing surface. Fact was, the usual chaotic mess around the place didn't much register, let alone bother him, when it was there; but now that it was all cleared away, the uncluttered room felt. . .well, it felt different. Better. Homey. He shook his head. *That doesn't matter. Just make the list and go bed down in the barn.*

⁂

The next morning, Miriam had already gotten up and set coffee to perk on the stove before he even reached the house. The aroma wafting from the oven promised something delicious for breakfast, and she cracked eggs into a bowl with the efficient moves of a woman accustomed to cooking. She wore a plain slate blue day gown, and a white apron covered most of the front of it. Not a ruffle, speck of embroidery, or ribbon adorned either garment.

"Good morning," she greeted him in a subdued tone.

Gideon looked at her keenly. Was she whispering because her head hurt, or was she trying to stay quiet so his brothers could snatch a few last minutes of shut-eye? Either way, she wasn't supposed to have shown her face yet. "You're still supposed to be in bed."

She simply cocked her brow askance.

"How does your head feel?"

"Not as bad today." She set aside the eggs and ladled a little hot water from the stove's reservoir into a bowl. Soon the yeasty smell of bread dough mingled with the other aromas. Gideon felt awkward, drinking coffee when she already had set herself to doing chores; still, it wasn't right to rob his brothers of the last bit of their sleep just because Miriam Hancock gave a rooster competition, racing for sunrise. He sat at the table and frowned. Someone had added several things to the bottom of his shopping list. Neatly penned as the letters were, he knew Miriam had taken it upon herself to get involved.

He squinted, then moved the paper a bit so he could read it more easily. *Tea, rolled oats, confectioners' sugar, cinnamon, nutmeg, oregano, paprika, curry, cloves, paraffin, pectin, four cards of shirt buttons, fabric—one half bolt white medium-weight cotton, one quarter bolt each of blue, brown heavyweight serge, and tan wool.*

"What's this?"

"It's a start. I'll add as I take stock of your supplies today. I can do without the curry and cloves if money is tight."

"You won't have time, Miriam."

"Time for what?" She sprinkled flour onto the far end of the table, dumped the bread onto the spot, and kneaded it with negligent ease. Dusted with flour, her hands still looked incapable of managing any but the simplest and lightest of tasks.

He cleared his throat and looked for a way to say what seemed almost cruel. "Hannah doesn't need your help anymore, Miriam. Your reason for coming no longer exists."

The heel of her hand sank into the dough, stretched it, then she pinched off a third of the big, fragrant, white blob. A few deft flips of her hand shaped a portion of it into a loaf. She made the second loaf and started to form the remaining dough into a third when she said, "If anything, the reasons I came are more pressing now than when Hannah first penned them."

"You can't stay."

seven

Miriam blinked at him and thought she'd misheard. The state of affairs in this household was so appalling, the very idea of this man shoving away her help didn't make a speck of sense. Then she reasoned out what he was saying. "Of course I can't stay in the back bedchamber and occupy your bed," she agreed crisply. She hoped her cheeks didn't go pink at the fact that she'd already ousted him from his bed for two nights. "We'll have to come up with an alternative arrangement at once."

"The arrangement," he replied, glowering over the rim of his coffee mug, "is for you to romp with the girls for another day or so, then go back home."

She set her hands on her hips, not caring that she'd leave flour prints on her apron and dress. Flour would brush off easily enough, but she. . .she would not be brushed out of this home as if she were a bothersome gnat. Gideon Chance had best understand here and now that she'd not back away from duty. She locked gazes with him. "I'm not going to sail back to the islands."

"Listen, lady, I don't know what whim brought you here, but it's nothing more than that: a whim, and a plum crazy one at that."

Her jaw hardened, and she did her best to keep a civil tone as she informed him, "My sister's needs for assistance constituted a clear need, sir."

"Hannah must've written on a day she was just a tad blue. A woman in her, um. . ." He glanced down at the tabletop and mumbled, "Carrying months is entitled to a melancholy day or two."

Miriam, too, looked down and messed with the second loaf. Its shape was a bit off, so she evened it out as she struggled to reply. "Had only one letter been melancholy, we'd have understood; but Hannah was always a cheery soul, and though she mentioned kind things, in all but the first two letters, she couldn't hide her loneliness or the fact that help was necessary."

He folded his arms on the tabletop and leaned forward. His tone went hot. "Well get this, and get it good, Miss Miriam: We live on a ranch. It's not fancy, and we're not rich. We can't afford servants, and every last one of us sweats hard for what we have. Your sister made Daniel a happy man, and he did right by her each and every day. This is a harsh land. If it was too brutal for your sister, it's going to be just as miserable for you. You'd best go now."

"No."

His jaw jutted forward, and his eyes lit with temper. "Women don't belong here."

"Fancy that. In case you haven't reasoned it through yet, my nieces will become women."

"By then, things'll change."

Miriam barely leashed her anger. She punched the bread dough and turned her back just long enough to grab the loaf pans. She'd already greased them, so she dumped a loaf into each one and silently recited the books of the Bible to help her keep her temper. She set the loaf pans beside the stove, emphatically shook out a dishcloth to rest over them, and finally turned back toward Gideon. "I'll stay. I'll help things change."

"Now hang on here."

"That is precisely what I intend to do," she cut in with an icy smile.

"It's not fitting—"

"Oh, I agree. It's not fitting for my nieces to be reared in a pigsty. They've not been taught to say grace, their hair is uncombed, and they'll certainly learn no table manners if left to your brothers' care."

"Now you just hold it right there!"

Miriam stared at him. "Your younger brothers were imbibing devil's brew within the tainted walls of a house of ill repute when I arrived. Don't for one minute expect me to entrust the impressionable hearts and souls of my sister's daughters to men who have no morals or manners. I won't. I can't."

"No one asked your opinion."

"Mr. Chance, I'm afraid you simply don't understand." She looked at him and shook her head. "Girls need tutelage and tenderness. They need social graces and spiritual guidance."

"Every last one of us can read and cipher just fine. Those girls won't lack book learning. As for tenderness, every last one of us loves both of them to distraction, so you needn't fret over that."

"But their manners and morals?"

The muscles in his cheek started to twitch. "Lady, you've got a heap of gall, barging in here and judging us."

"I didn't barge. I was invited."

"Yeah, but Hannah did the inviting, and she isn't—" His voice came to an abrupt halt.

Miriam sucked in a sharp breath and let it out very slowly. "Here anymore," she finished. Her voice carried a taste of the woe she felt. She paused for a moment, then said, "And that is precisely why I must stay. In honor of her memory and as a tribute to the very principles she held inviolate, it falls upon me to make sure her daughters are reared in an appropriate and decent manner."

"You can't stay."

"You've already said as much, but I'm afraid you'll simply have to reconsider."

"Daniel—"

"Is grieving. I understand that. I've already promised not to wear any of my sister's clothing."

"It's not just the clothing."

She nodded. "I know Hannah and I look—" She caught herself, gulped a big breath, then forged ahead. "*Looked* quite similar. Seeing me must have been a terrible shock for him. I'll wear my hair differently, and that should help."

"Only a woman would come up with a silly plan like that." He waved his hand in a gesture of disgust. "Applying that boneheaded logic, slapping a different saddle on my mare would make her—"

"You're not," she interrupted, "comparing me to a horse, are you, Mr. Chance?"

"Now don't go pitching a hissy fit."

"I'm not given to having fits, sir. You're addressing that comment to the wrong person. Daniel is the one who has let his emotions sway behavior beyond reason. Nevertheless, I understand grief is to blame, and I'll manage to deal with it. By and by, he'll become accustomed to my presence."

Gideon cast a quick glance at the closed bedroom door. Miriam understood why. The last thing either of them wanted was for this to turn into a shouting match. His brothers didn't need to overhear this conversation at all. His voice lowered to a growl. "This is his home. You make him. . .uncomfortable."

Miriam stopped and looked at him. For a moment, their gazes held. "Mr. Gideon Chance, this isn't about what makes your brother comfortable. We're all bound to be uncomfortable for some time. I'm scarcely accustomed to any of this myself, but this is not about adults' feelings—it is about children's needs."

"Polly and Ginny Mae have all they need!"

She shook her head sadly. "I'm afraid that simply proves my point. They are warm and fed, but the same can be said of your horses and hounds. Why, when I took the laundry down from the line last evening, Polly claimed the smallest man's shirts as her own dresses!"

Gideon's neck and ears went ruddy.

"At first, I could scarcely credit it, but then I took stock of the clothing, and I realized my niece was wearing the only dress she owns! Pardon me if I'm drawing the wrong conclusion, but as far as I can tell, you men let that little girl run about in a man's shirt. How could you allow such a travesty?"

"Travesty? It's no travesty. Bryce and Logan outgrew those shirts. It's shameful to waste."

"Shameful! Why, you cannot mean—"

"They serve Polly just fine." He glowered at her. "Besides, who's going to see her but us, anyhow?"

His assertions left her spluttering. The matter was far from closed in her opinion. He wasn't about to have her dictate his family's ways; she refused to leave her sweet little nieces alone with a band of barely civilized men. He folded his arms akimbo.

"Best you forget these opinions and wild notions about staying, Miss Miriam. For the next few days, you'd do well to rest. You're looking peaked, and that won't make for a very good voyage."

"Voyage?"

"Home," he asserted. His head nodded, as if to paint an exclamation mark in the air to punctuate his feelings. "We'll just trade in your return ticket for an earlier departure."

"What return ticket?"

eight

"What return ticket?" Gideon echoed for the dozenth time as he went out to work with the horses. He smacked his gloves against the fence post and tamped down the urge to bellow in outrage. He wanted to shake the teeth right out of Miriam's pretty head. How could she have come halfway 'round the world and planned to stay? Her father must be daft, sending her to Hannah. Hannah was only a tad bit older, so expecting her to shield Miriam from the real world and shelter her from harm was utter nonsense. In essence, they expected Daniel to shoulder that burden—but Daniel was in no shape to do so, and Gideon wasn't at all eager to fill those shoes.

"How much does a trip to the islands cost?" he wondered aloud. He moaned. Money was tight. Real tight. They had enough for provisions but not enough for frills. He yanked on his right glove. Faced with being strapped for another year or getting saddled with a prissy missionary's daughter, he'd go for the lesser of the two evils. Miriam would have to go—and soon.

Real soon.

Moments after his brothers had gotten up, they started grumbling. Paul finally stuck his head around the bedroom door. "Where the. . .uh, Titus and I can't find our shirts, and Bryce's britches up and disappeared."

"I'm responsible for the missing garments," Miriam confessed. Her tone was so conciliatory, Gideon knew he'd underestimated the scope of the problem. This woman had her heart set on staying, and she'd give in, make sacrifices, and bend over backward to convince his brothers that she belonged here. A shy smile flitted across her face as she continued. "When I took the laundry off of the line last evening, I kept out the articles of clothing that require mending. Could you possibly make do with what you have? I'll be sure to catch up on the mending today."

After Paul managed to shut his gaping mouth, he stammered, "That's right kind of you, ma'am. I mean, miss. We'd all be obliged. Much obliged. Truly. None of us is any good with a needle."

At breakfast, she set stuff on the table the likes of which Gideon and his brothers hadn't tasted in years. His brothers were voluble in their appreciation and approval. Mama loved to cook like this; Hannah had made fair meals but never much pushed herself past doing plain fare.

Miriam hadn't just scrambled eggs and made biscuits. She hadn't gone the extra step and whipped up a pan of white gravy. Oh, no. Miss I'm-Here-to-Stay pulled out all the stops. She'd chopped up bits of ham, onions, and tomatoes into the eggs. As if that wasn't enough to make all of their taste buds take notice, she opened the door of the oven and pulled out a pan of coffee cake. The aroma steaming off it had Gideon reaching for a piece as soon as she put it on the table.

An hour later, trying to forget about breakfast and concentrate on work, Gideon remembered the way she'd fleetingly rested her hand on his shoulder so she could refill Logan's and his coffee cups. Her touch had been innocent and brief as could be, but when she moved on toward Paul and Titus, he'd wanted to yank her back and check to see if he'd been imagining the sweet smell of flowers clinging to her.

Disgusted at himself, Gideon pulled on his left glove and

muttered under his breath, "Half-wits. My own brothers are a bunch of no-good, belly-rubbin' half-wits. If she thinks she's gonna buy her way into this family on our just-mended shirt sleeves or through our stomachs, she's got another thing a-comin'!"

Dinner reinforced her good standing with his brothers. She'd made corn bread and fancied up the beans she'd been soaking with hunks of side meat. She'd picked cabbage from the garden, sliced it into thin shreds, and mixed all sorts of stuff with it. The stuff could coax every last apostle out of heaven for want of a taste.

She didn't eat with them, either. She and Polly had held a tea party a short while earlier. While the men ate, Miriam lifted Polly up on a chair. The puzzling woman pulled a measuring tape from the sewing bag she'd brought in her trunk. Tan his sorry hide, Logan had unearthed a stack of feed and flour sacks, and Miriam went so far as to promise Polly she could choose whichever she fancied for her new dress. While she and Polly chattered like magpies about a pretty new frock, Daniel's eyes shot sparks that could ignite a forest fire. All of the other brothers lapped up the food like a pack of starving wolves.

Gideon knew he had to do something—quickly.

❧

Gideon stepped into the cabin for supper, unsure whether to anticipate or dread what was to come. Miss Miriam had missed her calling in life. The woman could plot until she had a man twisting in circles. Had she been born a man, she'd certainly have attended West Point and become a military strategist. *And that means she wouldn't have been sashaying around here, wearing that flowery scent and ugly dress and driving me half daft.*

"What have you been doing today?" Logan asked their little

niece as he tugged on the ribbon tying off one of her freshly washed, neatly plaited pigtails.

"Auntie Miri-Em fixed all of the shirts. She putted lotsa buttons on 'em. And she hided all of the holes so they all gone." She paused for effect, then hiked up the hem of the dress she was wearing to show off layers of white ruffles underneath. "Looky! Auntie Miri-Em maded me panty-lettes."

Logan let out a hearty laugh.

Gideon cast a glance over at Miriam. She'd turned back to the stove, but he could see the curve of her cheek. A rosy hue that hadn't been there moments before tinted it now.

Thoroughly entertained, Bryce let out a wolf whistle and waggled his brows. "Aren't you just the prettiest little fashion plate?"

"I not a plate," Polly huffed in obvious dismay. She patiently pointed at the table. "Plates is on the table. Panty-lettes is on me."

The way she hiked up her hem to display her fancy little girl drawers to illustrate the second part of her assertion was downright funny. Gideon chuckled under his breath.

Miriam cleared her throat and said in a slightly croaky tone, "Polly, you may come be my best helper now. Put the bread on the table."

"Goody!" Polly stopped making a show of her unmentionables and galloped over to her aunt. White ruffles stuck out from beneath her hem, making what had been a too-short-to-be-decent dress look acceptable. Gideon wouldn't admit he thought it looked utterly charming—even if it was kind of girly. He also didn't want to admit that once Polly was out of diapers, they hadn't bothered to put her into any undergarments. White's Mercantile sold men's long johns, but they didn't have a thing for kids. Asking Reba White to special order something for Polly was one of those awkward things that somehow managed to slip the Chance brothers' minds when they went to town.

Polly wound her arms around Miriam's skirts for a quick hug, then looked up expectantly. Miriam stooped and gave Polly a basket full of sliced bread. She murmured something softly to the girl, then asked, "Understand?"

"No," Polly retorted in her clear, high voice that carried well. She frowned at Miriam and tilted her head to the side. "How come a lady is 'posed to wear her panty-lettes, but she can't talk 'bout them? My panty-lettes is so pretty!"

That did it. Gideon succumbed to the temptation. He threw back his head and roared. Miriam looked so disconcerted, he couldn't help it.

Daniel sat off in the corner, glowering. Gideon wasn't sure whether his levity or Miriam's prissy ways caused his brother to look like he'd been sucking on lemons. Paying attention to his surly ways wouldn't change them. *It's a temporary situation,* Gideon told himself as he stopped laughing. *Miriam will be gone in no time at all.*

As if she knew what he was thinking, Miriam used all the strategy of a general and the wiles of a woman. She put supper on the table. Everything was done at the same time, and she managed to coordinate her moves so efficiently, she didn't get in a dither while juggling platters, bowls, and the like. In a matter of moments, rich, thick, my-mouth-died-and-went-to-heaven chicken stew and her light-as-clouds bread graced the supper table. A colorful dish with whacked-up tomatoes, cucumbers, onions, and bits of herbs looked like something a fancy chef would serve at an expensive San Francisco restaurant. How she managed to knock around in their kitchen and garden and concoct such mouthwatering meals was a total mystery. No matter who cooked, none of the Chance men ever managed to create anything half as appealing.

"Supper is ready, gentlemen," she announced.

Gideon wanted to wallop his brothers. She hadn't even finished the sentence, and they were falling all over each other to reach the table. He intentionally waited a minute before taking his customary place at the head of the table.

Titus sprang up, pulled out a chair, and said, "Here you go, Miss Miriam."

"Thank you," she said. . .or simpered. Gideon wasn't sure whether she was genuine in her gratitude or trying to wrap Titus around her little finger.

Miriam claimed Polly again. They folded their hands, and the brothers fell into a chagrined silence. They'd already started to dig in. Spoons froze halfway to mouths, then were lowered down to rest in the bowls as Polly's uncles heard the little tyke singsong a prayer all by herself. Good sports that they were, they all chimed in on the "Amen."

Daniel kept hold of Ginny Mae, but he had his hands full, trying to keep her from sticking her fingers into his bowl. Miriam reached over, scooted his bowl farther to the right, and grabbed a small tin plate from the center of the table. That plate had tiny bites of chicken, vegetables, and little fingers of buttered bread on it. They were all the perfect size for Ginny Mae to pinch with her chubby baby fingers and eat all by herself. Miriam set the plate down in front of the baby, but she said nothing.

"Well looky there," Bryce said. "Hannah used to do that for Polly."

Daniel's head swiveled sharply toward Bryce. His eyes burned like coals. Bryce stared at his brother for a long moment, then cleared his throat. "I do believe I need the butter for my bread." He jabbed Titus in the ribs. "Gimme the butter."

Gideon wasn't sure whom to kick under the table first: Daniel for being mean as a chained bear or Bryce for sticking his foot in his mouth yet again.

The plate was a good idea. He hadn't spied it because it was on the other side of a canning jar filled with wildflowers. The last time they'd had flowers in the house was when Hannah was still alive. She'd gotten a fistful of them and spoken wistfully about the big, fragrant blossoms back home. It hadn't occurred to him that she was homesick; but as he thought back, that would have been about the time she'd written to invite Miriam to come. Besotted as Daniel was, all of them figured he kept Hannah happy. The fact that she'd been carrying a second child so quickly certainly reinforced the notion she felt every bit as contented about her life and marriage as Daniel was.

Gideon paused, his spoon halfway up to his mouth. He'd not thought about Hannah for months. She'd been like a rainbow—pretty, but fleeting. Insubstantial. Foul as Daniel's mood had grown, if he knew his brothers were thinking of his wife, he'd have spoiled for a nasty fistfight.

As for Miriam. . .well, Gideon vowed to be sure she and her trunks made it on the very next voyage back toward her parents. At the moment, her luggage occupied a chunk of the floor over by the window. She'd pulled her outfit today from the larger of the two trunks.

An uncharitable thought arced across his mind. For being a pretty gal, Miss Miriam sure worked hard at looking homely. He'd held her. He knew her shape. It had plenty to recommend it to the opposite gender. Instead of fancying up that slate job with a lacy collar, fancy buttons, or doodads, she'd left it painfully plain. She'd proven she could wield a needle with great skill, so why did her gown bag a bit on her? Had she been ailing? Had she lost weight?

He sent the bowl of the fancy salad her way after taking a generous second helping. "You'd best eat up, Miss Miriam. From the way your gown fits, I'd guess you had a bit of trouble keeping your meals down on the voyage here. We'll need to fatten you up in the next few days 'til you leave."

"Leave!" Logan half shouted.

"You're going? Say it isn't so," Bryce said. To Gideon's disgust, his brother looked like a lovesick calf.

"I—"

"She has to go," Gideon cut in before Miriam grabbed the chance to put in her two cents' worth.

Paul scowled. "She just got here."

"Yes, I did. Since this involves me, I—"

"Ought to stay," Titus finished for her as he set down his coffee mug with a decisive *thump*. "It's downright cruel to stick her back aboard a vessel this quick. We've all heard how difficult a voyage is, and she's not even rested up and recovered."

Daniel glared at her. "She can lie in her berth day and night if she's all that worn out."

What little color Miriam's face held seeped away. "I refuse to be locked in a cabin for weeks on end again!"

"Locked in a cabin!" Logan and Paul bellowed in outrage together.

"Now, Miss Miriam," Gideon said through gritted teeth, "there's no need to stretch the truth here."

"Oh, I'm not stretching it one bit. Two days out of port, Captain Raithly locked me into the first mate's cabin. I didn't see sky again until the day we docked."

"He didn't do it unless you deserved to be punished," Daniel snapped.

Miriam recoiled as if his words packed a physical blow. Her eyes and voice radiated hurt. "Daniel, what did I ever do to deserve your judgment and condemnation?"

Daniel glared at Gideon and slammed his fist down on the table. "I told you to get rid of her."

Polly climbed into her aunt's lap. She managed to smear food across the slate bodice, and she clung to Miriam's sleeve. Tears slipped down her cheeks. "Please don't go, Auntie Miri-Em."

Miriam kissed Polly's forehead, then gave Gideon a pleading look.

The sight of her cuddling Polly close, the way she naturally smoothed and fingered her niece's little curls, the spill of dainty white ruffles on a child who had never owned anything frilly—they tugged at his heart. He and his brothers had somehow slipped up and not tended to some of the finer points of rearing a girl. *But now that we know, we can do it.*

"Auntie Miri-Em, I need you!"

"I'll stay just as long as you need me," she pledged.

"You're going," Gideon asserted. *How dare she invite herself, then announce she was going to move in and take over matters and make decisions?* That proved the point: Miriam Hancock had to leave before she tried to change and rule their comfortable world. "I said we'd buy the stupid ticket!"

"Gideon Chance, you'll watch your attitude and language!"

He glowered at her. "The last thing I need is some holier-than-thou, prissy, missionary girl telling me what to do at my own table."

Miriam let out a long sigh. "Very well. I'll give you options to fulfill that requirement. Either I'll take possession of the cottage and take my meals there—"

"Don't you step foot in my home again." Daniel's voice rivaled a thunderclap.

She lifted her chin. Her eyes didn't snap with temper, and her jaw didn't jut forward with stubbornness, either. Gideon had to give her credit, because her eyes didn't even well up with tears. For being a woman, she had remarkable self-control. "Since that choice does not suit, I'll simply take the girls back on the ship with me."

Daniel lurched to his feet with a loud roar. "No!" He kept hold of Ginny Mae in one arm and whisked Polly out of Miriam's hold with the other. "We don't want you, and we don't need you. Get out of here. Get out of our home and lives."

Bryce hopped up. "Don't you talk that way to her! If you wasn't holding the girls right now, I'd bust your chops."

Gideon had been on his feet and about to say something similar. He caught himself before he made a buffoon of himself. *Here I am, about to be her champion, yet I want her gone.* The sight of his smallest brother, a mere teen, standing up to a full-grown man angered him. "Enough of this. We're not coming to blows or having a brawl. I made a decision. It stands."

Awkward silence filled the room. Ginny Mae smacked her little hand over Daniel's chest. "Daddy, Daddy, Daddy."

Daniel's expression qualified as purely malevolent as he spoke to Miriam. "She knows whom she belongs to, and it isn't you." He turned to Gideon. "Get rid of her. Today."

They watched Daniel as he stomped to the door, went out, and kicked it shut with a vengeance. Gideon managed not to wince.

"Gideon," Paul said.

"What now?"

Paul folded his arms across his chest. That move always warned Gideon his brother was about to render an unwanted opinion.

"You're not going to drain our savings to buy Miriam's

ticket on a ship. You have no right to make that kind of financial commitment without consulting us."

"Yeah," Titus agreed. "We all do a fair share of the work. This is a voting issue."

"Excuse me, please. If you'll allow me a moment, I should absent myself from the table until this is settled." Miriam slipped from the table, took something from the oven, and set it on the table, then went out the door.

Gideon looked at the table and groaned.

nine

Gingerbread. Miriam had made gingerbread. Gideon's mouth watered as he said, "You're Daniel's brothers and owe him your support and allegiance. He loved the daylights out of Hannah. He doesn't want to be saddled with her kid sister. It's a big responsibility, and we're all doing far too much already."

"She helps, Gideon," Bryce said in a wheedling tone. "She cooks and cleans and watches the girls. She's not a burden."

"The girls need a woman's touch," Paul said thoughtfully. "Dan's not making any bones about how upset he is, but Dan is. . .Dan. He'll get over it."

"You're not sure of that at all," Gideon countered. "He carries a grudge worse than a gypped cardsharp."

Logan shrugged. "Tough luck. You got a good gander at Polly. We love her and Ginny Mae to pieces, but Miriam's already doin' things for her we can't. Seems to me, as time passes, it's going to be more important to have a woman around to tend to female-type matters."

"That's years down the road," Gideon countered. He tried like anything to ignore the aroma of the gingerbread. "By then, one of us will probably have married."

"And is Dan going to buck like a bronc then, too?" Bryce asked. "It's been ten months since Hannah passed over. I'm not saying that's all that long, but I do think he'd better learn he has to go on living. He's not thinking of his girls—he's thinking of hisself."

Titus cleared his throat. "You asked us to think of Daniel, Gideon. Well, I am. I think we have to save him from himself. All of us already stepped in and helped with those girls because he can't do it all on his own. This is another one of those times when we're going to have to intervene."

"Think this through. Where in the world does she sleep? What in thunder are we going to do with a single woman underfoot?" Gideon realized it sounded like he was weakening. He immediately tacked on, "No, it's all wrong. She has to go."

"That's your vote," Titus said. "We all know where Daniel stands on this. I say she stays."

"She stays," Bryce and Logan said in unison.

Gideon turned to Paul. "Don't vote until you think this through. I didn't make a snap decision. I've been thinking it over from the very start."

Rare were the times things came up for a vote. Gideon usually made the decisions. Because he shouldered that responsibility, they'd agreed if a vote ever came to a tie, he'd make a final determination. If Paul voted for Miriam to go, it would be a tie, so Gideon's decision would stand. If Paul sided with the others, they'd be saddled with a fussy little snip of a woman until she, too, sickened and died.

Paul was the quiet brother. Thoughtful. Did more reading. His cautious nature had stood them in good stead more than once. He ambled to the windows—the windows Miriam had cleaned—and looked out. "Have you ever wondered what it would have been like if Mama died instead of Dad? We'd have kept the old ranch, but that old ranch house would have felt so empty. Mama made the house a home. Even here, rough as this was, she set out her quilts and stuck wildflowers on the table. Hannah did that, too, and it did us all good."

And Miriam's already started nesting like a sparrow, too.

Gideon glanced at the colorful bouquet on the table.

Paul turned back around. "Polly and Ginny won't remember their mama. There aren't three decent women within a day's ride. Someone's got to teach them to pick posies, cook, and quilt."

"If we couldn't keep Polly in drawers and a dress," Logan said, "we sure won't train her or Ginny Mae up so they'll be good women."

Gideon groaned. *This is a nightmare!*

"Gideon's right," Logan said. "There's gonna be plenty of trouble, keeping her here. Dan's likely to splavocate. Furthermore, we're not gonna be able to shower in the rain or talk without censoring our words."

For a second, Gideon perked up. *The tide might turn. Logan's changing his mind.*

A breath later, Logan dashed his hopes by finishing his thought, "Then again, with the girls gettin' older, those things would have to come about sooner or later, anyhow."

"Let me grab the bull by the horns," Gideon said. "If you're worried about the money—"

"Yeah, money is another consideration," Paul admitted. "We've got enough to see us through. We've already lost one ranch 'cuz Dad borrowed on it. We know he paid back the money, but bankers are good about losing vital papers, and I don't trust Pete Rovel over at the bank."

"Nuh-unh," Titus chimed in. "Not any more than I'd trust a riled polecat not to spray. We empty out the account to buy a ticket and have even one disaster, and Pete's going to own this ranch."

"You're not saying anything I haven't already thought."

"Let me give you one more thing to consider." Paul looked back out the window. "Miriam doesn't want to go back. I doubt it's because life with her parents kept her miserable. Hannah constantly reminisced about how perfect everything was back on the islands."

He swung back around and stared at Gideon. "Miriam was locked in her cabin the whole voyage here. Think about how plum-outta-her-mind scared she was of us at first. How she fought and reminded us it was a sin. Locking her up was cruel as could be, but it was the only way the captain could protect her. She doesn't realize just how lucky she was that he kept her imprisoned. It's been years, but Dan still won't say a word about what went on aboard the ship when he was shanghaied. It was a harsh life for him, and he's a strapping man. What kind of men would we be to put her—a lone, pretty, tenderhearted woman—back aboard a ship full of the dregs of mankind?"

Logan gloated, "The vote stands four to two. Miss Miriam's stayin' put."

Gideon accepted the vote. Though he didn't want the responsibility of having a woman around, his brothers were more than right—the babies needed a woman's touch, and sticking Miriam back on a ship would be a low-down move.

He left the house and wasn't sure where to look for her. The woman didn't have a place to go. He craned his neck to see the graves, but she wasn't there. Since he'd found her in the garden once before, he headed back there. Though the garden lay empty, Gideon spied her sitting on a corral fence. He strode over to her.

Miriam didn't bother to turn around. She hunched forward and had her arms wrapped around herself. The evening air felt a trifle chilly. Gideon scowled. "You left without your shawl."

She nodded in acknowledgment.

"We'll see how things work out, but for now, we'll let you stay."

Slowly she turned to look over her shoulder at him. Even in the meager moonlight, he expected to see her gloating smile. Instead, she looked somber as a priest. "I'll do my best to help the girls and stay out of your way."

That was what he wanted her to say. Why didn't it make him happy to hear it?

"Could you please tell Daniel I'll try hard to avoid him?"

He nodded. "We'll knock together a cottage for you. It'll be about a week before we can get to it, though. Someone's tacking blankets to make a space for you so you can sleep closer to the stove and be warm enough in the meantime."

"Gideon?"

"Yeah?"

"I'm sorry I chided you about your language in front of the others. In the future, if I have a problem, I'll try to speak to you privately."

"Fine. It's too chilly out here for you. Go on inside."

❧

The next morning, Miriam hastily put her hair up into a respectable bun. After tying the blanket-curtain out of the way with a bit of twine, she set to work. She stoked the fire, had coffee going, and fried her own ham and egg. She'd finished her meal and had the rest of the eggs all scrambled and ready to cook before any of the men came out of the bedroom.

They sat on the benches around the table and yanked on their boots. Miriam had already filled both pitchers with hot water.

Logan started to take the pitcher back to the bedroom.

"Logan," Miriam called softly, "in the islands, the men almost never wear shirts. The bedroom is already crowded, else you wouldn't have had the washstand out here. I'm not offended if you men shave here."

She turned her back on them and finished cooking breakfast. Two at a time, the brothers washed and shaved. Boot scuffle, razor scrape, a chuckle, a splash, and a mixture of Bryce's silliness and Titus's early morning grumpy responses filled the cabin.

Miriam caught sight of Gideon's black eye and gasped. The set of his jaw and the way he stared at her dared her to comment. She bit her lip and turned away. *I came to help my sister, but I'm turning brother against brother.* She swallowed hard, then took her lead from him. If he wanted to pretend nothing had happened, she could play that game. . .up to a point.

Miriam set the meal on the table, then took the egg basket and left. She hoped Daniel and the girls would slip in during her absence. She also prayed the other brothers landed on Daniel so he'd behave. Bad enough he was nasty to her; he had no call to take his temper out on Gideon.

After all, Gideon didn't want her here any more than Daniel did.

❧

Waking up to the smell of coffee and sizzling ham posed no hardship. Walking out to see a comely woman at the stove struck Gideon as pleasant enough. The matter-of-fact tone she used in commenting on shirtless men astonished him, seeing as she acted downright shy with his brothers most of the time. Come to think of it, he was the only one she ever looked in the eye. Miriam Hancock seemed more puzzling each day.

The sick look on her face when she saw his black eye let him know she was a sympathetic woman. Intuitive, too, since she'd not breathed a word about it. He hoped she wouldn't say a thing to Daniel.

Daniel didn't show up for breakfast at all. Polly skipped in all by herself. "Daddy said we get a picnic. Somebody's 'posed to put breakfas' in a basket."

Gideon turned to the side so the little one wouldn't see his shiner. Paul stepped up to block the view. "You skip right back and tell your daddy someone will bring the picnic in just a jiffy."

Bryce stuck food in a crate and carried it to the door. Gideon ordered, "Tell Dan he shows up and sits at the table, or he doesn't eat. He'll act civil, too."

A rascal's smile lit Bryce's face. "I don't expect that's going to be much of a problem for very long. Cold eggs and a jar of colder coffee won't suit him one bit."

"What about the coffee cake and ham?"

"I reckon the rest of us forgot Dan hadn't gotten his portion yet. It's all gone."

"I see."

"Yeah. Does Dan's face match yours?"

Gideon shook his head once, decisively. "Not with the babies around. One of us had to be smart enough to stay in control."

It was Daniel's day to watch the girls. The rest of the brothers got to work. Gideon rode out and inspected fences. No need to keep an eye out for trees they could fell to use for Miriam's cottage—Dan's way of handling his anger and grief had been to chop down trees and keep them in firewood. An enormous pile of logs was stacked behind the barn—more than enough for Miriam's cabin and to expand the barn to twice its width.

Thinking of a cabin for Miriam tightened Gideon's jaw. He'd been outvoted, and he'd live with the decision. But he didn't have to like it. Being responsible for a woman—and a bitty one at that—didn't set well. He'd been careful to make sure that, though they didn't eat fancy foods, the girls always had plenty of good healthy meals, sunshine, and thick blankets. They were hearty little snippets, but accustomed to tropical weather and an exotic diet, Miriam didn't have the same physical reserve. Maybe he ought to put a little potbelly in her cabin. That way, she could make some tea during the winter to warm up from the inside out, too. Besides, a little stove would save them the time of collecting stones and building a fireplace.

By chance, he spied Todd Dorsey. Though neighbors, they often didn't see each other until they went to town. Todd tipped back his hat. "Heard tell you've got Hannah's sister visitin' and she's quite a looker."

"Miss Hancock is spending time with her nieces."

"You could be sociable and give me an invite for supper. A woman's cooking and company would be welcome." The whole time he spoke, he studied Gideon's shiner. "Must be a real pretty sight if you men are coming to blows over her."

Gideon hitched a shoulder.

"She visitin', or is she stayin'?"

"For the time being, she's staying. You can pass the word that we'll be raising a cabin for her come Friday."

"Friday, huh? That's quick."

"Chances were never men to jaw around when work needed doing." Gideon jerked the front of his hat brim lower on his forehead and rode off.

Todd Dorsey's interest served as fair warning. Men in Reliable were woman-hungry. The storekeeper and his wife had a daughter of marriageable age, but they were the only decent women in the whole of the township. The rest of the place consisted of men struggling to tame enough land to finally bring families out or to start a family, but the greatest number of men fell into the latter category. They'd gotten squared away enough, and they were itching to have a decent meal and a dainty missus.

"I'll get Paul to put a steer on the spit. Barbecue's decent enough meal," Gideon muttered to himself as he squinted toward the house. "As for a decent missus, the men are going to have to search elsewhere. I'm going to have to watch out for that obstinate woman until she finally sees reason and decides to go back where she came from."

❧

"Men coming Friday." Gideon bit into a rib and tore off a big hunk of meat with his teeth yet still managed to add on, "Building a cabin—a little one."

Miriam barely kept from dropping the bowl of mashed potatoes on the table.

"No need to." Daniel glowered at Gideon. "This is a very temporary situation."

"You never could tell time." Gideon shot him a smile, then took another bite.

I've managed to set brother against brother. That fact made Miriam seek a way to make peace between them, but she knew she was the worst person to intervene. Gideon wouldn't appreciate her meddling, and Daniel wanted nothing to do with her, let alone her opinion.

Bryce stuck his elbow on the table and rested his sandpapery chin in a sauce-splotched hand. "If you two was dogs, I'd knock your heads together and dunk you in the trough to cool you off."

Logan grabbed a rib from Daniel's plate and bit into it. "I'd help him. I'd hold you under longest, Dan. You got some nerve, coming to the supper table and eatin' a woman's good cookin' when you're speaking ill of her."

"I didn't say anything about her at all." Daniel reached over and swiped back the rib. He scowled at the missing chunk.

"She has a name, and you'll use it." Gideon's voice rivaled a thunderclap. "You'll help build Miriam's cabin, too."

"Daddy, Auntie Miri-Em maded me pretty panty-lettes. Are you going to make her a pretty house?"

"Eat your supper, Polly."

It didn't escape Miriam's notice that Daniel avoided answering the question. She served herself a small dollop of potatoes and passed them on.

"Daddy says we don't get 'taters very much 'cuz they used them all to make our fireplace." Polly smiled at Miriam. The rib the little girl had been nibbling from the center had hit both sides of her cherubic cheeks, painting her face with clownlike charm.

"Your fireplace?"

Polly nodded. "Daddy picked them out of the ground and piled them. Up, up, up!" She raised her messy little hands high. "Mama made gravy and poured it over the 'taters, then Daddy built a great big fire."

"Imagine!" Miriam could scarcely fathom Daniel concocting such a tale.

"Turned those potatoes rock hard," Bryce chimed in.

"So no one can take a nibble out of them." Gideon gave Polly a pointed look and shook his head from side to side.

Her little head wagged in agreement. "We gots to leave the 'tato stones all alone."

Miriam looked from brother to brother. Daniel glowered at her, the rest looked rather sheepish, but Gideon—he simply gazed into her eyes. She said, "A grand fireplace like that would warm hands and hearts."

Gideon's lips relaxed into a heart-melting smile.

"Unca Gideon, how come you didn't wash your face? Auntie Miri-Em says we gotta wash 'fore we eat."

"It's an ouchie."

He told the truth, but he didn't implicate Daniel. Gideon's an honorable man.

"Auntie Miri-Em kissed my ouchie finger today and maded it all better." Polly licked her finger and held it up to prove her point.

Bryce and Logan started to snicker.

Polly pointed at Gideon's eye. "Ask Auntie Miri-Em to kiss your eye all better."

Gideon's brows rose. He turned toward Miriam.

He wouldn't. He couldn't.

The corner of his mouth took on an impish slant. "Well, Miss Miriam?"

ten

The man is a rascal. Miriam handed her napkin to her little niece. "Polly, you should kiss your uncle better. Here. Wipe your face first."

"Why? You're closer." Polly gave her a puzzled look.

Gideon's brothers all started to chuckle—well, all except for Daniel. Daniel finished ripping the last bite of the rib from the bone and concentrated on his plate.

Mortified, Miriam stammered.

"It's not going to hurt anything," Paul said in a stage whisper.

Miriam rose from the table. "Does anyone else want more coffee?" Just as she turned away, she brushed a fleeting kiss on Gideon's temple and scampered to the stove, sure her face was hotter than the coffeepot.

Mirth filled Logan's voice. "Gideon'll take a refill, but he's had all the sugar he needs now."

Gideon cleared his throat. "Sugar's on the list of supplies we need. I'll go to town tomorrow. Anything anyone needs?"

❧

"Whaddya doin', Giddy?" Bryce flopped down on the back porch. Within seconds, two dogs and the barn cat all vied for his attention.

Gideon surveyed the yard and continued to stare at it. "I'm making plans."

"Plans for what?" Bryce scratched Nip between his ears.

"A cabin."

Bryce's face lit up. "You weren't kidding. I hoped not. Tell

85

me—you gonna marry Miss Miriam?"

"Whatever put that foolish notion in your head?" Gideon glowered at him.

"Well, we built a cabin for Daniel when he married up with Hannah. I just thought you were lookin' to have a place to share with your missus, too."

"I'm not marrying her." Gideon fought the urge to add on to that assertion.

"If you ask me, that's a crying shame."

"I didn't ask you."

Bryce proceeded to check the hounds' ears for ticks. As he tilted his head to do the job, he drawled, "Miss Miriam's a fine cook and does a right nice job with the girls. Seems to me, somebody ought to marry up with her so's she doesn't get stars in her eyes for some other fellow and leave us."

The notion of not having to worry about Miriam appealed to Gideon, but the notion of her falling in love with anyone gave him indigestion. "None of the men hereabouts would be suitable for a lady like Miss Miriam."

"You tryin' to convince me or yourself?" Bryce got up and dusted off the seat of his britches.

Gideon ignored the question. "While I go to town today, I want the area between Daniel's and the house leveled. It needs to be ready for Friday."

"Fair enough."

After Bryce sauntered off, Gideon recalled last night's supper. His brothers were big teases, and Hannah never appreciated their rowdy ways at the table, but Miriam didn't seem upset in the least by chuckles and jibes. . .except when it came to the kiss. The gal's face went redder than a cardinal when Polly asked her about the kiss. *I don't know what came over me, letting the joke go on.* But Miriam didn't get snippy. Light and quick as a butterfly, her lips grazed his temple, and she'd flitted off. *The gal has gumption.*

Titus's early morning growl of a yawn and Paul's deep chuckle came from inside the house. Threaded among those was a foreign sound. Gideon strained for a moment, then closed his eyes as the hymn Miriam sang so quietly reached him.

"When darkness seems to hide His face, I rest on His unchanging grace. In every high and stormy gale, My anchor holds within the veil."

Paul joined in, "On Christ the solid rock I stand. . . ."

Gideon couldn't recall the last time anyone sang. Well, yes, he could. Titus had a habit of humming and whistling—but not singing. Hannah used to hum to Polly every now and again. Before that, Mama sang. In fact, she had a special fondness for this particular hymn. Mama couldn't sing worth two hoots. Miriam actually made listening a pleasure. Come to think of it, Paul had a decent voice, too.

Funny how even after not having heard this hymn for years, Gideon still recalled the lyrics. He had plenty to do, but he just stayed put and let the song play out.

The door to Daniel's cottage opened. Polly scampered across the yard, her hair a tangled mess. *I wouldn't have noticed that fact before Miriam came.*

Daniel held Ginny Mae and strode over. She seemed a mite unhappy, and he kept patting her on the back. "If you're going to town, get some paregoric. I can't tell whether she's teething or colicky, but she was up half the night."

"Breakfast is ready," Miriam said from the kitchen door. Polly already clung to her skirts, and Miriam tentatively reached for Ginny. "Food's on the table. Why don't you go ahead and enjoy a hot meal?"

Shifting Ginny to his other side, Daniel clipped, "Only takes one hand to eat." He shoved past Miriam and went inside.

"Daddy gots two hands," Polly said as if it were an important fact.

"Yes, he does." Miriam playfully tapped her on the nose. "So do you, and yours need washing before you eat."

Gideon went to the table and gave Daniel a dark look. This situation was going to come to a head sooner or later, but now wasn't the time. Paul bowed his head and said grace. It was short and to the point, but it was the first time any of the brothers had communed openly with the Almighty in well over a year.

Forking four thick slices of French toast onto his plate, Gideon declared, "This smells terrific."

"Do we got bacon today?" Polly climbed onto her chair. She poked at the bacon on her plate. "Daddy, see? It's not burned."

Daniel's face remained impassive.

A few minutes later, Polly shoved her plate away. "I don't like it. It's yucky."

Everyone looked to Daniel to handle his daughter's rudeness. He simply picked up his coffee and took a long swig.

"I like it just fine." Gideon reached over, speared a bite from her plate with his fork, and ate it.

"Me, too." Titus and Paul did likewise.

"I want sumpin' else."

"What you're going to get," Gideon said very quietly, "is time in the corner. Naughty little girls aren't allowed to sit at the table."

"Auntie Miri-Em sits at the table. Daddy said she's bad."

Abruptly all movement and noise ceased at the table.

"We're all bad sometimes," Miriam said tentatively. She took a shallow breath, then continued. "Jesus understands. We tell Him we're sorry, and He forgives us."

"That's enough." Daniel bolted to his feet. The brusque action set Ginny to wailing again. He glared at Miriam. "Now look what you've done."

Miriam stood and walked around the table. She barely came to Dan's shoulder, and Gideon stood behind her, ready to intervene.

"You're tired, Dan. I overheard you tell Gideon she kept you up much of the night. Polly probably didn't sleep all that well, either. I'll take them for the day. Why don't you go nap?"

Nonplussed at her gentle offer, Daniel stared at Miriam. He'd been spoiling for a fight, and she'd just knocked the wind right out of his sails.

"You don't know a thing about babies." His hands closed more tightly around Ginny Mae, and her squall made it clear she didn't like it one bit.

"I helped Mama with sick calls, and a doctor came about the time Hannah left. I often assisted him. I daresay I can handle a fussy tot." She reached up and took possession of Ginny. Dan didn't look all too certain about turning loose, but he did so.

Miriam smoothly pivoted and slipped away. She crooked her forefinger. Ginny gnawed on it and hushed. "There we are," Miriam murmured as she carried the baby toward her own bed and laid her down. Nothing short of admiration flooded Gideon as Miriam continued to let little Ginny Mae chomp on her finger as she used the other hand to lift the baby's gown.

"Your daddy thinks it's your teeth or your belly. Let's find out."

The moment she alluded to Daniel, Gideon turned toward his brother. A series of emotions flashed across Dan's face—anger, grief, worry, resignation. Miriam hadn't challenged his authority or faulted him in any manner. She'd simply offered to lighten his burden, and in moments like this, Gideon realized how deeply burdened and troubled his brother had become. *As long as she can deal with him, I need to keep my mouth shut. I won't have him hurting her, but she's got a backbone of steel and a heart bigger than the ocean she crossed to get here.*

"Daniel, some babies get diaper rashes when they teethe." Miriam reclaimed her finger and deftly unpinned the diaper. "Has Ginny Mae gotten one when she got any of her other teeth?"

Miriam acted as if she'd had a dozen of her own young 'uns. She knotted the corner of a dishcloth, dipped it in syrup, and let Ginny gum on it. That seemed to help some. By the time Miriam scorched flour and used it on Ginny Mae's rash, the baby hadn't quite regained her usual sweet disposition, but she'd sure enough stopped sounding like someone was trying to murder her.

Daniel groused around the table for a few more minutes, then took his leave.

"Gid said we're to level the land for Miriam's cabin," Bryce announced.

Miriam's head shot up. She gave Gideon a startled look that slowly changed into a grateful smile. Not that a missionary's daughter ought to know how to play poker, but Miriam best not ever try. Her face tattled on every emotion she had. Endearing, that quality.

His brothers all vacated the house and set to doing their chores, leaving behind a table stacked with dirty dishes. Soapsuds, splashes, and wadded towels festooned the washstand. Polly squirmed worse than a calf getting branded as Miriam plaited her flyaway hair. Saddling Miriam with this mess didn't seem quite fair. Come to think of it, Hannah used to try her best to wrangle a ride to town whenever one of the brothers went.

Gideon cleared his throat. If ever there were a time they needed Miriam to help with the girls, surely this was it. A fretful teether wouldn't allow more than a few moments' peace all day. Polly didn't often become peevish, but when she did, she could try the patience of a saint. Both girls would be at their worst.

"You don't have to mind the girls. It's Paul's day. If you wanted, you could ride in to town with me. Reliable's not fancy, but—"

Miriam started laughing as she tied a scrap of twine around the end of the braid. "Go, Gideon. I'll make the trip some other time. I'd like you to post a letter for me, though."

"To your folks?"

She shook her head. "It's too costly to do that just yet. I'll wait a few months until we settle in. I'm sending a letter to my grandmother. It's a bit heavy, but she'll be able to forward an enclosed note to my cousin, Delilah, since I'm not sure where she's living now."

"I'm more than happy to post whatever you write. Are you sure you're not coming to town? It might be a long while before you have a chance again."

She looked up at him and shrugged. "You have the list, don't you?"

"Yeah." He shifted uncomfortably. "Your sis—she always hankered to go along."

A bittersweet smile crossed Miriam's face. "I can imagine. Hannah loved adventure. Me? I'm content to stay wherever I settle."

❧

Late in the afternoon, Miriam heard footsteps on the porch. "Wipe your feet!"

"Yes'm."

She didn't bother to turn toward the door. In fact, she didn't want to. Her face must be red as a hibiscus. Instead, she toed the runner on the cradle to keep Ginny Mae from yowling and continued to sew.

"Done?" Polly asked for the hundredth time.

"In just a minute."

"I reckon you'd like the provender on the table so you can squirrel it away wherever you want." Gideon plopped a heavy crate on the table.

"Unca Giddy, did you bring me candy?"

"Just a minute, Polly. I need to bring in more stuff."

Miriam took advantage of the seconds when he'd be outside to push in her escaping hairpins and tuck straggling strands of hair behind her ears. Her apron bore splotches of syrup, coffee, and smashed yams. It hadn't bothered her for the other Chance men to see her in such disarray. *But they want me here; Gideon doesn't.*

Yes, they wanted her here. That fact came through clear enough. Loud and clear—as they all argued on where to level the ground for her cabin. Each had given thought to the location.

Paul and Titus said it ought to be close to Daniel's cottage since she'd be minding the girls. Daniel woke up to the noise and bellowed that they were to build it next to the main house. Logan figured halfway between might be smart so she could go either way in bad weather. Bryce wasn't sure whom to listen to, so he'd just hitched up horses and started dragging a huge log from one building toward the next. They'd leveled the whole area and come inside for lunch—every last one of them filthier than any man Miriam had ever seen. It took her a full hour just to scrub the grime from the house.

Scraping sounded. "I'm wiping my feet again." Gideon's

voice held more than a hint of teasing.

"Do I get my candy now, Unca Giddy?"

"In a minute, tidbit. Mind if I set the material on your bed, Miriam? I don't know where you plan to store the bolts."

"Go ahead. Thank you for getting them." She started to tie a knot in the thread.

Polly danced from one foot to the other. "You done now?"

Miriam got ready to clip the thread. "Your dolly will be ready in just a minute."

Shoulders drooping with an exaggerated sigh, Polly whined, "How many minutes do you got?"

Gideon started to chuckle.

Miriam snipped the thread and quelled the smile that fought to break free. It would be easy to indulge Polly, but part of the reason she was staying was to teach her niece basic manners. "Remember how we talked about turns today?"

"But I don't wanna wait. Can't I pick when it's my turn?"

"Nope." Gideon grabbed Polly, lifted her high above his head, and jostled her. "Everyone waits for things—even you."

"Why?"

Miriam knew she'd remember the startled look on Gideon's face for the rest of her life. He didn't have a single notion on how to answer that question.

"Because you're a big girl," Miriam said. "Big girls can learn things because they are smart. You're smart enough now to learn how to wait for your turn."

"She's not just big. She's huge. I can barely hold her up anymore." Gideon pretended to drop her. Polly shrieked in delight as he caught her midair.

"Auntie Miri-Em is making me a dolly. It's a toy, and she'll be my very own little baby. Wanna see?"

Miriam gave the doll to Polly. Gideon hunkered down and

volubly admired it. "Now will you look at that? Isn't she a beaut?" When Polly wandered into the other room to tuck Dolly into one of her uncle's beds, Gideon straightened to his full height. His features went somber. "I never thought about a little girl needing a doll. I don't think she's ever seen one."

"It's just an old shirt sleeve I salvaged. I'm sure when she's a bit older, Daniel will be sure she has a nice one."

"Don't sell yourself short. That rag doll is all a little girl could ever want."

His words warmed her heart.

"Perhaps I'll sew some clothes for her doll. Daniel could give them to her for Christmas."

"You'll give them to her yourself."

He really does plan on me staying here. Christmas is six months from now.

Gideon gave her a wry smile. "Yes, I understand what I just said. I reckon you're here for keeps."

Miriam reached around to retie her apron strings. She barely held back her laughter. "It took you long enough."

"Now wait a minute. You're the one who thought you wouldn't be here for Christmas!"

"I thought nothing of the kind." She flashed a smile at him. "I already planned to make Polly a new outfit as my gift."

eleven

Thursday at lunch, Miriam set a basket of rolls on the table and smiled her thanks as Gideon pulled out her chair. "How many men do you expect to come help build the cabin tomorrow?"

"Can't say for certain."

Paul crowded into his place. "Us, maybe eight more. I'd venture probably a dozen or so all together."

Titus nodded. "Sounds about right to me."

Gideon took his place and folded his hands. He gave Miriam a nod, and she said grace. The Chance brothers didn't do a whole lot of talking at the table during the midday meal. They tended to shovel in as much food as they could in the least amount of time possible. Miriam had learned that sketchy plans for the day comprised any breakfast discussion and all conversation usually took place at supper.

Still, Miriam needed to ascertain a few basic facts. "Will those eight men eat as much as you all do?"

Gideon gave her an amused look. "Stop fretting. We're putting a steer in the fire pit."

"Bunch of nonsense," Daniel groused. "Practically reenacting the Prodigal Son, killing the fatted calf." For all of his bluster, he still gently spooned a bite into Ginny Mae's mouth. "Built my cabin without anyone else coming by."

"This way, it'll only take one day," Logan reasoned.

"Paul and I'll saw the floor planks this afternoon." Gideon sopped the last of the stew from his bowl and popped the roll into his mouth. "Bryce, make sure the troughs are full for everyone's horses tomorrow."

Titus rested his elbows on the table. "You haven't said anything about the plans yet."

"No need. Same as Daniel's." Gideon rose.

"Auntie Miri-Em, you better start making gravy for the chimney!"

Miriam started to wipe Polly's hands.

Gideon cleared his throat. "No need. I have White bringing a little potbelly stove from his mercantile."

"Great galloping hoptoads!" Bryce blurted out. "Really?"

"Yep." Gideon strode toward the door as if he couldn't escape fast enough. His voice went gruff. "You all get to work."

Titus was the last to leave. He tarried by the door a moment.

"Did you need something?" Miriam asked.

He gave her a lopsided smile. "I'd be happy to pick a couple of heads of cabbage so you could make that fancy cabbage salad." Once he'd built up the nerve to make that request, he added on, "You'll have to hide it from Gideon, though. He'd eat the whole bowl of it before anyone got a chance at getting a mouthful tomorrow."

"It needs to stay cool, Titus. I'll make it tomorrow."

"Make it today. I'll put it in a bucket and lower in into the well. Hovering stuff above the water keeps it chilly as can be. Ma used to do that to keep food."

"Wonderful! Thank you."

&a

"Every last man in Reliable township is here," Paul marveled the next morning.

Gideon growled and called himself twelve kinds of an idiot. Of course the men came. Miriam was single. Pretty. Could cook. He'd hoped a few men who could spare a day's labor would get a quick peek at her today, then leave her be. He'd planned on them spreading the word that Miriam belonged to the Chance family and wasn't looking for a husband.

So much for my grand plan.

White's wagon rolled into the yard. Gideon let out a grateful sigh. Reba had come along. She'd help Miriam in the kitchen and keep any of the fellows from getting too friendly. As he helped Reba down from the wagon, she gawked about. "Looks like half the world came."

Bryce counted aloud. "Thirty-seven, Giddy." His eyes went wide. "That's more than three dozen!"

And every last one of them is hovering near Miriam, trying his best to capture her attention. I've got to do something.

Reba tugged on his sleeve. "I'm going to borrow Logan and Titus to help carry those crates inside. I figured Miriam would need some help feeding the hordes."

Gideon cast a quick glance at the crates and gave Reba a relieved smile. "You're a peach."

Daniel had a daughter in each arm and stomped up as his other brothers emptied the wagon. "I'm taking the girls to my cabin and shutting the door. This is a circus, and I'll be lucky if they don't get trampled. I hold you accountable for the whole mess. You've got enough men here to build a dozen houses!"

Gideon watched his brother slam the door to his cottage, and a slow smile lit his face. *Maybe not a dozen, but. . .*

He cleared his throat. "Men!"

They stopped palavering and turned toward him.

"Thanks for coming out. Fact is, a whole lot more of you showed up than I planned."

"Folks ain't gonna think you're so smart anymore, Chance," Chris Roland hollered. "Everybody knows you got a pretty gal up here. 'Course every man jack in the county came!"

The men hooted with laughter.

Gideon hooked his thumbs in his belt. "Well, they're gonna think I'm right smart all over again, then, because I'm going to take advantage of your strength. Daniel's been chopping down trees for months now. I figure we can organize into groups and put up *three* cabins today!"

"You ain't smart. You're plumb crazy!"

"Then Chris," Gideon said, pointing his forefinger at the man who called out that insult, "it seems to me that your team ought to be able to beat mine."

"You're on! I'm calling Rusty on my team."

"Wait—" Rusty yelled. "What does the first team done win?"

Gideon paused a moment. He turned when he felt Miriam's light touch on his arm. She stood on her toes and whispered in his ear. He nodded and announced, "Sunday supper. Miss Hancock will cook Sunday supper for the winning team."

The men all shouted with glee and quickly organized themselves into three teams. Gideon turned to Miriam and gave her a stern look. "You stay right by Reba White. I don't want these men troubling you, and she knows how to handle them."

"You don't have to worry about me, Gideon. I had to deal with all of the sailors back on the islands."

Her innocence made his blood run cold. "Those sailors wanted sinful union and likely found it in any number of brothels; these men want a wife. You're the only prospect around."

"Then you'll simply have to tell them I'm unavailable. I'm committed to rearing my nieces."

Reasoning with Miriam was as preposterous as saddling a squirrel. Gideon hollered, "Reba? Will you come here?" Reba marched on over. "Do me a favor. Keep the men away from Miriam."

Spurred on by the prospect of eating Miriam's Sunday supper, the men worked with zeal. The simple square floor plan with a door in the front and a window in the back made for rapid construction. All of the men had built their own cabins and worked together to raise barns. When they set to business, they knew what they were doing.

Then again, each team seemed to have notions as to what would improve the basic plan. Gideon's team built on the foundation that had the floorboards in place. Clearly that would become Miriam's. They wanted to put an additional window by the door, so they set the door one third of the way across the front instead of dead center.

The middle team, under Chris Roland's lead, determined they had a better plan. Their cabin featured a front and a back door—and Rusty was busy making dutch doors so each one could become a window if the occupant so chose.

The cabin closest to Dan's started out exactly like the plan. Paul was leading that team. He and Titus kept quiet, but Gideon could tell they were up to something by the way the men would huddle every now and again to discuss something. Sure enough, they kept on building the walls higher while men braced the first two cottages' roofs.

No one wanted to stop since Miriam's Sunday meal hung in the balance, but she banged a spoon on the bottom of a pot. "Gentlemen, I'm calling a break. It's only fair everyone cease laboring for the same length of time."

They grumbled good-naturedly and headed for the food. Daniel came out of his cabin, and Polly ran toward Miriam. "Auntie Miri-Em, I get to eat first! It's my turn because I already washed my hands and face. All the men gots dirty hands. See?" She held up her little pink scrubbed hands.

Gideon sat on a stump and watched as big, burly men all

backtracked and waited by the pump so they could sluice off. He suspected this was the cleanest some of the men had been in ages. *Miriam probably thought the same thing of us when she arrived.*

Bryce stood over by the pit with Logan. They started slicing off slabs of meat. Men piled it high on pie tins, then went toward the table. Miriam and Reba had cooked up a storm. Good thing, too. He'd thought Miriam overdid when she'd had eight loaves of bread and four pies last night. With two score men, that wouldn't be sufficient. Truth be told, men would be satisfied to load up on the barbecue, but they'd feel cheated if they didn't get their fill of sweets. *Thank the Lord, Reba brought pie, too!*

Gideon caught himself. He'd been thanking the Almighty quite a bit lately. In truth, ever since Miriam showed up and just lived her faith in the simple, straightforward way that she did, he'd been reexamining his own ways. He'd found a whale of a lot to be grateful for and had become a whole lot less irritable.

Society matrons would swoon, but practical Miriam did what needed to be done with what she had on hand. Two two-gallon wooden buckets held potato salad and the cabbage slaw salad he liked so much. Deviled eggs, pickles, and tomato slices made the table look restaurant-fancy. Not only were there baskets of sliced bread, but also plenty of drop biscuits. Best of all, eight pies lined a board the women laid over two barrels.

"Whaddya have there?" Todd Dorsey called.

Reba rested her hands on her hips. "Two dried apple pies, two peach, a custard, two chocolate pudding, and a shoofly."

A masculine chorus of groans and satisfied grunts filled the air.

"That isn't all. Miriam made oatmeal cookies."

Marv Wall elbowed his way toward Miriam. "That does it. I'm not doing another lick of work. I'm proposing marriage so Miss Miriam won't need a cabin here."

Gideon was ready to wring Marv's neck, but Miriam clapped her hands and laughed. "Oh, that was the best joke I've heard yet today, sir. You simply must have the first choice of pie for having such a charming sense of humor."

Marv got a bewildered look on his face. Gideon took pity and bellowed, "The ladies better cut the pie else he'll take a whole one to himself!"

"I'm not averse to having a pie of my own, but I'd rather have the cook," Marv said mournfully.

"The cook," Miriam singsonged, "is here to take care of her nieces. I'm sure you gentlemen understand, and I'm thankful that you're here to help me settle in with my family."

"Guess that says it all, men." Gideon took a stance by Miriam and stepped out in faith. "I aim to ask a blessing on the food." The yard went quiet. Gideon's pulse thundered in his ears as he bowed his head. "Almighty God, we give Thee thanks for the fine things in our lives—for land and livestock, family and food. Draw us close to Thee, we pray, and bless the hands that prepared the meal. Amen."

"Amen," the men said in unison.

He gestured toward the food. "Dig in." Miriam said nothing, but she'd slipped her hand in his as he prayed. It felt. . .right. Like it belonged. His heart felt right, too. Like he'd come home—not just because they were of one accord, but because he'd been keeping the Lord at a distance and that had changed.

The men made utter pigs of themselves. It wasn't until every last speck of food was gone that they decided it was time to start up on the challenge again. "Paul and Titus are going to take forever to get that third cabin done."

"We'll see about that!"

Axes rang out and saws grated. Men counted as they worked in accord to heave logs into place. Gideon's men went back to the far pasture to fetch more logs for the roof. He dusted off his hands and stood back to survey the progress.

His cabin for Miriam would be sound. It still needed chinking and a window set into it, but those things didn't take much time or effort. It would be a fine little place, and he'd even kept some of the scraps from the floor planks and hammered them together to make a drop leaf to serve as a writing desk that folded against the wall.

The center cabin sat square as could be, and it got a mighty fine breeze going through with both doors wide open.

Gideon surmised what Titus and Paul were doing and gave them a nod of approval. Instead of making a peaked roof, they'd built up the front and left the roof as a simple downward slant to the back. The extra height bore support trusses for a loft.

Paul sauntered over and swiped his sleeve across his damp brow. "Dan and the girls'll outgrow their little cottage in a few years. Titus and I decided we might as well bump it up a bit."

"Good thinking." Gideon looked at the three new buildings with a growing sense of satisfaction and slapped him on the back.

Bryce mopped at his neck with a bandanna. "This is the workin'est day ever." His sunburned face split into a smile, and he elbowed Paul. "Couldn't have done it if Dan hadn't been in such a foul mood and hacked down so many trees."

Paul and Bryce started laughing.

"Men," Miriam said as she daintily picked her way across chips of wood and bark. She smiled at them. "I'd like a word, if you will."

"Better make it quick," Gideon warned. "Don't want to slow down our teams."

Miriam's eyes sparkled. She reached them and looked from Gideon to Paul and Bryce, then back at Gideon again. "The men have all worked so hard. Would you mind terribly if all of them came for supper after church?"

Gideon toed the dirt and shook his head. "Miriam, there's a problem."

She turned a becoming shade of pink. "Oh dear. I'm sorry. I didn't think about how much food—"

"That's not the problem." He sighed. "Sweet pea, other than an occasional itinerant Bible-thumper who happens through, Reliable doesn't have a church."

She looked utterly flabbergasted.

"Maybe it's not quite that heathen," Paul added hastily. "The last one said he's riding circuit and will be back through every other month or so."

Her mouth opened and shut a few times. Then she smoothed her skirts. "Well, we'll just have to remedy that. It's summer, and the weather is lovely as can be. We'll have worship right here in the yard."

She turned around and sashayed back into the house.

Bryce got a stricken look. "Giddy, do something!"

Gideon shrugged. "You did this. You voted for her to stay, and now she's changing everything. Live with it."

twelve

"Everything's changing," Miriam murmured to herself with delight. Over the last few weeks, she'd settled into her new cottage, tacked up cheery yellow feed sacks as curtains, and braided a small rug to go by her bed.

She'd taken shameless advantage of the big move. When Paul and Titus moved into the loft cabin, she washed their tickings and had the men stuff them with fresh hay. Gideon now occupied the middle cabin. He'd seen to his own bedding, and instead of leaving his doors open all day long as did his brothers, he kept his shut. Logan and Bryce now shared the big bedroom in the main house. Miriam suspected Bryce smuggled one or more of the dogs in there each night, but she said nothing.

As soon as she'd arrived, she'd expanded the garden. Polly loved to "help," and Ginny Mae relished crawling in the dirt. The biggest challenge was keeping her from eating bugs, worms, and rocks. Polly wore pantalets and simple smocks made from feed sacks instead of hand-me-down shirts. Sweetest of all, she now said prayers.

"Breakfast about ready?" Paul called to her as she stepped out onto the porch. He'd been heading toward the chicken house.

"I need the eggs!"

"Come help."

She lifted her skirts a bit and skipped across the yard. Back home, there was more sand than dirt, and it took considerable effort to get anywhere. Here, the packed earth made for ease of travel. These men had no concept how fortunate they were to live without the ever-present irritation of sand. Grit from the beach got into every nook and cranny. Dust could be wiped clean; sand never departed.

Paul slid a bolt free and looked down at her. "Might want to stand back a shade. The hens can be pecky after being shut in all night." He swung two six-foot-high doors open, revealing dozens of boxes full of nesting hens.

"This is like a kitchen cupboard!"

"Yup." Gideon rested his hands on her shoulders. Miriam had heard him coming. She knew the assured sound of his no-nonsense stride. She fought the urge to lean back into his strength as he explained, "Mama designed it. None of us liked stooping to fit into the crowded, dirty coop. Paul, Speck is off her feed. Bryce is having a look at her."

Paul hastened toward the stable. Miriam started gathering eggs, and Gideon reached the nests that were up high. Quickly they filled the basket. "I didn't mean to have him strand you with his chore."

"I kept chickens on the islands. I don't mind."

"You already do plenty around here."

Miriam slipped her hand beneath a pullet and admitted, "Life here isn't easy, but it's good. You men work hard."

He snorted. "We get filthy and eat like ravenous beasts. I still don't understand why you'd choose to live here and deal with us."

Miriam hitched her right shoulder. "It seems to me, no matter where they live, men lose buttons, tear shirts, rip knees, and bleed. Back home, Mama told me a woman's mending basket and laundry are bottomless. I'm not complaining."

"Miriam!" Logan called from the house. "Todd Dorsey

came to see about a horse trade. Mind if he stays to breakfast?"

Neighbors stopped by with astonishing frequency—and always at mealtime. Gideon never seemed very pleased about those social calls. He bristled. "Yahoos and clods. Ever notice these mooches just so happen to turn up at mealtime?"

Miriam laughed. "I think it does them some good, seeing little Ginny Mae and Polly with all of you big, strapping Chance men. Plain as can be, those little girls need a woman's touch, and I'm the only woman around."

The muscle in his jaw twitched. "That's all they notice, Miriam—you being a woman." He stomped toward the house, and Miriam mentally dismissed Todd from the breakfast table. No one ever managed to get something past Gideon. *Except me. I'm the exception that proves the rule, because I'm staying here.*

Gideon. Once he'd accepted that she was here to stay, he'd stopped acting as if he'd been invited to his own execution. Responsibility rested heavily on his shoulders, and he took it seriously. But she wanted to be sure Gideon understood she wasn't another responsibility—she was. . . *What am I?*

Helpmeet was the first word that came to mind, but that was all wrong. It meant she was his wedded wife. She wasn't a partner. Neither was she a maidservant nor a relative. Miriam resolved not to label what she was but instead to concentrate on how she would lighten his load and insure her nieces' ultimate welfare.

Led by Gideon's example, most of the other Chance brothers embraced her presence with ease. Some days, it seemed as if she'd been here forever.

Miriam carried the egg basket into the house. Daniel sat on the floor, struggling with a knot in the lace of his boot. Miriam set down the egg basket and handed him a fork. "Try this. The tine can help you tease it loose."

He nodded and kept his head bowed over the stubborn tangle.

Daniel seemed to be changing, too—but slowly. Instead of being surly or belligerent most of the time, he now stayed silent. Miriam removed a stove lid and shoved in another log as she mentally gave Hannah's husband credit for the love he bore his children. He cherished both daughters to distraction and showed them great tenderness. Because their welfare was his first concern, he'd grudgingly accepted the fact that Miriam would now play a role in their upbringing.

"Oh!" Miriam jerked away from the stove and started beating at the flames on her left sleeve.

"Here." *Whoosh.* Something wrapped around her, and Gideon was part of it. He held her in tight confines and rubbed her arm. "I've got it. You're okay. Titus, get the water pitcher."

Miriam rested against Gideon's chest and stared off to the side. Plates, mugs, and silverware dappled the just-swept floor. *But I set the table.*

"Quick thinking," Titus said as he hastened up with the water pitcher from the washstand.

"Here. Let me take a look." Gideon stopped rubbing and tried to twist her.

Miriam couldn't help herself. She burrowed closer.

"It's all right, sweet pea."

"Of course it is," she said. "I'm just cold."

"How can you be cold?" Logan slanted her an odd look. "You were on fire."

While Logan reminded her of that dreadful fact, Gideon managed to tug on her. Miriam wiggled, then looked down. "That's our only tablecloth! It better not—"

"Hush." Gideon finished unwinding her and proceeded to

yank what was left of her sleeve clean off her dress. "Pour the water on her."

"At least let me put my arm over the sink."

Gideon made an impatient sound and glowered at Titus. Titus immediately emptied the entire gallon of water over her arm. As the last few ounces slid over her, Gideon ordered, "Now let me see how you look."

"It's just a little burn."

He looked at her arm and carefully turned her hand so he could see more of her forearm. Miriam reached over to cover the center of the sizable pink splotch with her other hand, but Gideon smoothly manacled that wrist and turned his attention toward her injured palm. "We'll wait to see if you blister. Hopefully we caught it before the heat went that deep."

"Truly it's nothing much. My dress took the brunt of it."

"Not much of a loss, if you ask me." Logan picked up the charred remains of the sleeve. "I don't mean you any insult, but that dress is ugly as a mud-stuck fence."

"It was serviceable." *Serviceable*—a word she'd learned in her youth.

"Came out of a missionary barrel, didn't it?" Gideon's voice carried a healthy dose of disgust.

"Well, I—how did you know about missionary barrels?" As soon as the words left her mouth, Miriam regretted asking. "My arm's fine. You men must be starving."

"You sit down. We'll keep a cold compress to your arm. Dan, scramble some eggs. Logan, pick up the dishes."

Miriam watched in dismay as Logan took the plates and shoved them back onto the table. "I need to wash those!"

He used his sleeve to wipe away a speck. "No need. You just swept this morning. Fact is, afore you came, lots of the time, we didn't wash the dishes."

Gideon hovered during breakfast, changing the cool compress on her arm and buttering her bread. "I'm taking Miriam into town."

"I need to change."

"No, you're not." Gideon made the pronouncement as if it were chiseled in stone.

"I can't very well saunter about in polite company in a shredded gown!"

"Town isn't polite company."

Fifteen minutes later, Gideon tucked the shawl around her shoulders as the buckboard jounced toward town. "Listen here, Miriam. You're not a missionary's daughter anymore."

"Of course I am. Just because Daddy and Mama are overseas doesn't change the fact—"

"You're Ginny Mae and Polly's aunt. Ugly day gowns like this don't teach them to be ladies. Part of the reason you're here is to teach them the feminine side of things, and you're traipsing around like a penniless waif in a servant's castoffs."

She smoothed her brown skirts. "Serge is durable and—"

"Homely as mud. Tell me, why did Hannah show up with feminine colors? I remember her dresses being pink, and they had doodads."

Miriam smiled. "The rose-colored fabric came in a barrel. I made that as her honeymoon dress. Papa couldn't very well insist that her gowns be somber when she was celebrating her marriage."

"Well, we're getting you material in town. You're gonna sew yourself a fancy pink dress."

"Gideon, I can't. I promised I'd make myself look different from my sister."

"Dan can go fly a kite. You already pile your hair up on your head so you don't wear a bun at your nape like Hannah did.

Besides, your hair's warm like the sun and hers was pale. I don't want you thinking I'm being too personal or being harsh, but Hannah—well, she had two babes in three years. Betwixt them, she never did trim down. Dan must've been sun-blinded when he first mistook you for your sis. It's high time you stopped trying to waltz on eggshells to please him and did what you want to make yourself happy."

Miriam smiled at him. "But Gideon, I am happy."

"No, you're not. You're just accustomed to being content with settling for scraps."

&

Sunday arrived. Men came and sang hymns as best they could remember, though the lyrics took on more creativity than Miriam had imagined possible. Titus scrounged up a guitar Miriam hadn't yet seen and proved to be quite talented. Gideon read from the Bible about letting your light shine, and Chris Roland stood up and spoke from his heart about living a "God-fearin', devil-forsaken life." Paul rose to say a closing prayer, and Rusty hollered, "Tack on thanks for the grub. We're hungry and want to belly up to the table straightaway."

Miriam didn't look, but she suspected Gideon fought to keep from chuckling. As soon as Paul finished the prayer, she hastened into the kitchen. Gideon hadn't let her near the stove to cook anything earlier this morning. She'd prepared each pot on the table. Then a Chance brother had transferred it to the stove. Now, Gideon carried every last pot back to the table.

Soon she was dishing up meals and handing a filled plate to each man as he walked in from the back door and left through the front. Succotash, rice, roast, and gravy. The banker, Pete Rovel, came through for thirds.

"That Sunday supper did it," Logan moaned five days later.

Each and every meal, they had callers. The men avidly listened to the Bible stories Miriam told the girls. They seemed even more interested in what Miriam planned to put on the table.

By Friday, Gideon glowered at three visitors and sent them packing. When he turned to the table, his eyes narrowed. Miriam kept posies on the table all the time, but they were always wildflowers from a patch here or there around the property. Three yellow roses filled the jar today.

"Marv Wall brung them for Miriam," Bryce tattled.

Gideon looked at his brothers and drummed his fingers on the table. "Miriam, you need to put the girls to bed tonight."

She gave him a baffled look. Daniel insisted on tucking his daughters into bed each night. *What is Gideon up to?*

&

"We've got to do something. I don't want these men to keep calling on Miriam." Gideon paced in the barn.

Logan beat the heels of his scuffed boots on the bale of hay he sat upon. "She's workin' herself silly, cookin' for them."

"She's cooking anyway," Paul pointed out. "To my mind, it's more a matter that we can't afford to feed all of Reliable."

"Rusty had her writing a letter for him yesterday, and Dorsey talked her into mending his stinkin' socks," Gideon rasped. "She's not their wife. They have no call, counting on her to do those things."

"She does it for us," Titus said quietly.

"I can write my own letters!" Bryce objected. He then muttered, "Just don't have a body to mail stuff to."

"I told you letting her stay here was a mistake." Daniel glowered at them all. "You didn't listen. Now you have a peck of trouble, and I want no part of it." He turned and walked out of the barn. The door shut with great finality.

"If that don't beat all." Logan scowled. "Betcha he's going

straight back into his cottage and sending Miriam scurrying away."

"The last thing she needs to know is that we're talking about her." Hay shifted and whispered under Gideon's boots as he continued to restlessly measure the length of the barn. "Roses. Marv had to go clear into San Francisco to bring those to her. It's serious."

"I told you, you ought to marry up with her, Giddy." Bryce folded his arms across his chest. "Seems that one of the Chance men ought to."

"Dan's excluded," Paul said at once. "He's hurting too bad, and it's not fair to Miriam."

"And," Titus continued in the same vein, "we have to rule out Logan and Bryce because they're just plain too young. That leaves you, me, and Gideon."

"I reckon it's necessary." Paul cracked his knuckles. "Not my first choice, but definitely doable. I'm willing to draw straws for her."

Titus started to chuckle as he took three strands of straw and handed them to Logan. "Seems pretty hilarious to me. After all, our name is Chance. I've got a one-in-three chance of snagging a bride—and a pretty one at that—without having to fuss with getting all duded up and making a fool of myself, going courting."

Gideon gritted his teeth as Logan lined up the straws and broke one far shorter than the others with a flourish. Anger coursed through him that his brothers would concoct such a "solution" to this problem. "You're all out of line."

Logan shrugged. "You're the one who always tells us to think things through. Someone's gotta marry up with her. Why not one of us?"

"Because she's family, not a brood mare." Gideon stared at

them. "You don't treat a woman like this!"

"Nothing much is changing. She's already willing to stay and work," Logan reasoned. "And we all like her just fine—well, all of us but Daniel."

"Daniel doesn't like anybody," Bryce tacked on.

"If anything, we're truly making her family instead of a free maid." Paul nodded at Logan. "Let's get on with it."

Logan positioned the straws in his fist and held them aloft. "Who's first?"

Gideon swiped all three straws from his brother's hand, cast them down, and ground them beneath his boot. "I won't have it. No one's drawing straws for Miriam's hand. A woman deserves to be courted and cared about."

Titus leaned back against a post and shoved his hands into his pockets. A lazy smile tilted his face. "So. . .you volunteering, Gideon?"

thirteen

"Here. I've got it." Gideon nudged Miriam to the side and hefted the kettle of oatmeal. He thumped it onto the center of the table.

"I'm fine, Gideon. Truly." Ever since she'd burned her arm, he'd hovered over her. That day when they went to town, he'd bought material for two dresses for her—two! As if that wasn't enough, he'd gotten the one and only bit of lace Mrs. White had in the store. Each time he was in the house and Miriam got near the stove, he acted antsy. "Gideon, that little burn is long since healed."

"Nonsense." He swiped the coffeepot from the stove and headed back to the table. "You got singed from your wrist to your. . ." He made a slashing mark across his own upper arm.

Miriam let out a silent sigh of relief. It wouldn't have been proper for him to mention her elbow or upper arm. He and the older brothers seemed a bit better about such matters. Bryce and Logan often said things that weren't suitable for mixed company.

"She's kept it hidden 'neath her sleeves. Even if it was hurting, I doubt she'd tell us." Titus sat down to the table.

"You can show me, Auntie Miri-Em."

"It's fine, Polly. Now would you like butter and sweetening in your porridge or cream and cinnamon?" Miriam thought she'd successfully steered the conversation in a different direction until breakfast was over and the men headed out to work.

Gideon alone remained. He waited until she'd wiped Ginny

Mae's sticky face and put her down to crawl, then he towered over her.

"Did you need something?"

He gave no warning. With surprisingly nimble fingers, he unbuttoned her cuff and started to carefully roll up her sleeve.

"Gideon!"

"Don't get all prissy on me. You roll up your sleeves to wash dishes and do laundry." He ruched the sleeve higher and made an exasperated sound. "It's still red."

"Auntie Miri-Em's arm isn't all better?"

"Not yet, dumplin'."

"I know why."

Oh boy. She's going to blab about what I've been doing.

"Why?" Gideon didn't look at his niece. His blue eyes narrowed and grew icy as he stared at Miriam.

" 'Cuz nobody kissed her better."

"I'm a big girl. I don't need—"

"Of course you do. You kissed me all better when my eye was hurt." Gideon took hold of her hand and lifted it. Instead of planting a quick peck on her hand, he slowly turned her hand over and brushed his lips on the inside of her wrist.

Miriam gasped and tried to pull away.

Gideon kept hold. "Still tender, sweet pea?" Instead of letting go, he pursed his lips and blew across her wrist. "There. That'll make the sting go away."

"Unca Giddy? That maded Auntie Miri-Em's face get all burny-red."

"Tell you what, half-pint. I'll lift you up. You kiss one cheek, and I'll kiss the other. Think that'll make Miriam all better?"

"Oh, I'm fine. Just fine." Desperately Miriam tried to make her voice sound breezy, but it came out in nothing more than a croak.

Gideon ignored her protest. He scooped up Polly and held her out to give Miriam a kiss. Miriam leaned forward, figuring she could play along this far. Polly gave her a sloppy peck and giggled.

Though Gideon put their niece down, Miriam was stuck because Ginny Mae was clinging to her skirts. "Virginia," Miriam said, stooping at once to lift the unsteady toddler. "Come on up here."

Gideon crooked a brow at her, then glanced at Ginny Mae. "You've got things topsy-turvy, Miss Miriam. Usually kids hide behind a woman's skirts."

His words echoed in her mind as he walked out the door. Miriam wasn't sure whether to be relieved or disappointed.

❧

By suppertime Miriam still hadn't managed to think through the situation. She'd pulled weeds in the garden with a vengeance, hoping that might relieve the tension. Ginny Mae and Polly got so filthy "helping" her, she had to bathe them both. Grinding meat, then squishing it to make meatloaf only managed to weary her body. Her mind still returned to how Gideon kissed her wrist after breakfast.

It was the oddest thing. Gideon had acted. . .well, different. Attentive. Since the day she arrived, Miriam had appreciated what a stalwart man he proved to be. Dependable. Good-hearted. Rough around the edges but hardworking. Then, too, after she scratched the surface, she'd come to understand he feared the Lord and did his best to live an upright life. *Is he paying more mind to me, or is it just my imagination?*

The Lord knew the desires of her heart—a husband and a family of her own—but the way things had worked out, those didn't seem to be in His will. She figured she would become a spinster aunt to little Polly and Ginny Mae. *I'm doubtlessly making a fool of myself. Gideon was just being kind, and I could ruin what's turned out to be a pleasant arrangement. I won't get to wed anyone, but least I can count myself blessed to have a man like Gideon to champion me and to have these darling little girls to rear.*

All during supper, she tried to act normally, but sitting next to Gideon made her nervous. Finally he wrapped his arm around her shoulders and held her still. "Stop popping up and down like a jack-in-a-box. If someone wants something, he can just go fetch it for himself."

"But I'm in a chair; everyone else is on a bench."

"Forget it," Gideon ordered.

"Yeah, Auntie Miri-Em. It's your turn to forget. Unca Gideon had his turn to forget already today."

"What did I forget?" Gideon gave Polly a look of mock outrage.

"You was 'posed to give Auntie Miri-Em a kiss. Look—see? Her face is all burny-red again. Hurry up and kiss it all gone."

Mortified, Miriam couldn't imagine a more awkward situation. Every last Chance at the table stared at her—not that she could see anything more than the napkin she crushed in her lap, but she felt their stares all the same. Bryce and Logan were hooting. Titus snickered, and Paul seemed to be choking back laughter. Daniel—he huffed like a ready-to-charge bull. Worst of all, Gideon. He dared to crook his forefinger and hook it beneath her chin.

I'm not going to look at him. I can't. I won't.

His nearness enveloped her, and warm lips brushed not her cheek, but the arch of her cheekbone. Miriam forgot how to breathe.

"Stop messing around," Daniel growled.

How she made it through the rest of the meal, Miriam didn't know. Rattled, she managed to put applesauce on her mashed potatoes instead of gravy—not that it mattered much. She couldn't seem to eat more than a few bites. Daniel took the girls off to their cottage as soon as he gulped down his last bite, and Miriam practically raced out to her little cabin on his heels.

She lay in bed and stared at her cabin. The fancy, scrolled, wrought-iron bedstead creaked as she rolled to her side. All three dresses hung neatly on pegs Bryce had whittled for her. The washstand held her toiletries and a water pitcher and bowl. The little drop-leaf desk lay open, its support chains gleaming dully in the beams of moonlight that sneaked through the gap between the top of her window and the top of the feed-sack curtain.

Beside her Bible on the desk lay a handkerchief—a used one. She'd come to her room, seeking solitude and solace. Confused by her response to Gideon's really-nothing-to-it kiss, she sought wisdom from the Word of God, only to end up in the last chapter of Proverbs.

Why, God? Why did I have to read about the qualities of a good wife? I thought I'd accepted my spinsterhood. You know how much I adore Ginny Mae and Polly. I even have this sweet little home of my own. Instead of feeling grateful, I feel empty. Lonely. How can I feel so alone when I'm surrounded by these rowdy men? How could I possibly sense such a lack when I have Gideon's friendship? Was this how Hannah felt? She had a husband, but she was so unhappy and restless. Help me, heavenly Father. Help me accept what I do have, to praise Thee for the life Thou hast set before me, and to exercise gratitude instead of this sadness. Amen.

❧

"Something wrong?" Gideon stepped closer to Miriam at the sink as they did the breakfast dishes. She'd been subdued today.

She shook her head.

"If you're mad about that little kiss at the table last night—"

"You never told me how my sister died."

Gideon set down the plate he'd dried and draped the dish-cloth over his shoulder. *So that's what's troubling her.* He leaned against the cupboard and hooked his thumbs in his belt. "I didn't realize that I hadn't given you the details. Sorry if it's been bothering you."

"I've wondered."

Her confession sounded almost tentative, and Gideon decided he'd give her the truth as simply and gently as he could. "We don't have a doctor here. Reba came to help Hannah with the first birthing; she was back East, putting her daughter in a fancy finishing school, when Ginny Mae was born. Dan—well, he did his best. Hannah pulled through, but she never perked up afterward. Fact is, she stayed abed for almost three months. A doc came through and said she had the 'punies.' He prescribed a tablespoon of black strap molasses followed by a belt of rum twice a day, but Hannah wouldn't do it. She didn't suffer, Miriam; Hannah just faded away in her sleep."

Tears streaked Miriam's face. Hands wet with dishwater, she tried turning her face to the side and brushing her cheeks against her shoulder to dry them.

"Feelin' blue, sweet pea?" He dried her tears with the corner of the dishcloth. A thought shot through him and made him look at her more closely. "Are you ailing? Is that why you asked—"

"No. I–I just needed to know."

"Well, I think you ought to have a few days to ease off on work." She opened her mouth, but he pressed his fingers to her lips. "We already laid Mama and Hannah to rest, Miriam. Women aren't fashioned for this life. Remember me warning you of that?"

She spread out her arms, shook her head, and spun around. "Do I look feeble to you, Gideon?"

He looked at her shimmering green eyes. Miriam was the picture of good health. In fact, she looked better each day—far better than when she'd first come. The sun had kissed her cheeks, making them a fetching rose color. Never had he seen such a vibrant woman. Contentment and energy radiated from her.

"We're not taking any chances." He'd do everything in his power to be sure she stayed this bright and healthy. "You'll just have to rely on my judgment here. Today you just nap and stitch some fancywork—nothing essential. Maybe tat yourself some lace or something."

Gideon knew the minute he turned his back, she'd do a chore. He inspected a knife she'd just washed. "I'll get a whetstone and sharpen this while you tat." Pleased with himself for coming up with a way to keep her company and have her relax, Gideon nodded. It didn't take much to concoct a plan to court her.

Once he got going, he liked the opportunities that slipped into his mind. He didn't want to woo her with his brothers hovering around. Having them watch each step he took and judge every last word out of his mouth just plain didn't settle well. He could swipe her away and start to sweeten things up a mite so she'd start warming up to the idea of marriage. Pleased with his decision, Gideon announced, "Tomorrow, I'll take you into town so's you can have a visit with Reba."

"I just—"

"Tell you what. I'll teach you how to drive the buckboard tomorrow. That'd be grand, don't you think?"

❧

Grand doesn't begin to describe this. Gideon smiled to himself the next day as he sat so close to Miriam on the buckboard seat that a blade of grass wouldn't fit between them. He had his arms about her in order to guide her hands on the traces. She'd washed her hair last night, and the little wisps of wind-blown hair teasing his cheeks were soft as could be.

"I think I can do it." Miriam fidgeted.

"I'll let you drive on your own after we make it around this next curve." Gideon wasn't in any hurry to stop holding her close. Still he needed to mind propriety. If they pulled up to the mercantile with her tucked this closely to him, Miriam's reputation would be ruined. He cleared his throat and braced her left hand. "There's a nasty rut just at the bend."

"Oh. Thank you."

She's a sweet armful of woman. Tenderhearted, hardworking, and sweet-spirited. Marrying up with her won't be a hardship at all.

"You'll have to show me how to hitch the horses next time, Gideon."

He looked down at her. "Not that you couldn't, sweet pea, but there's no need. One of us will see to that task."

"The horses are beautifully trained. I imagine it wouldn't be very difficult."

"Bryce need only work with a horse a day or two, and it's a dream. He's hopeless with people, but with beasts, he's a wonder."

"God gives us all different gifts."

Her smile could make the sun look dim. "You always look on the good side of things?"

"Most of the time." She shrugged, and the action only served to remind him of his hold about her. "Bryce has a heart of gold, and he's never shy about volunteering to help out. He needs some direction, but that's just because he's yet a boy. He'll grow out of his awkwardness and into his manhood."

"He's halfway between grass and hay." Gideon sighed. "Some days, I wonder if he'll ever mature." The wagon rounded the bend, and Gideon slowly let go of Miriam. He didn't want to, though.

"He will. So will Logan."

"From your lips to God's ears."

Matter of fact as could be, she nodded. "I do pray for each of you every night. I trust in the Lord, Gideon—but I also trust you. Believe me. They'll become remarkable men. You're a fine example."

⁂

Boom! The rifle kicked so hard, it threw Miriam back into Gideon's vast chest. Had he not been bracing her, she would have ended up in the dirt.

"Well," he drawled from over her shoulder as he continued to hold her, "you just drilled some gopher a nice new hole."

"You saw where it went?"

"Yeah. I keep my eyes open. It's a helpful trick you might want to try."

The rifle grew far too heavy to hold, so she lowered it.

"Hey, now." Gideon stepped around and frowned as he watched her rub her shoulder. "That recoil can be nasty. Why don't we change over to something lighter? Pistols, maybe."

"Pistols?" she squeaked. "Gideon, those are for killing people."

"We already talked this to death, Miriam. My brothers and I have been working farther from home, and if a snake slithers into the yard, you'll need to protect the girls."

"I could just take them inside."

"Sweet pea, you scare the ever-lovin' daylights outta me. What did you do back home with snakes?"

Though she wanted to continue rubbing her sore shoulder,

she stopped. "There weren't any snakes on the islands."

"Oh, so it was paradise before the fall, huh?"

Miriam shook her head. "Not at all. Between the natives and the sailors, it was like Sodom and Gomorrah. That's why God placed us there—so we could let our light shine."

"Your light?"

"From Matthew 5:16. 'Let your light so shine before men, that they may see your good works, and glorify your Father which is in heaven.' The islands are full of darkness, Gideon. They need the light."

"But you came here."

"I did. The day I left, Daddy told me that my light would shine wherever God placed me. He and Mama are where the Lord intends for them to serve, but they'd prayed and felt God had someplace else for me to be." She looked around them, then back into his deep blue eyes. "I feel as if I've been sent to paradise."

"That's a tough one to swallow. Hannah always spoke of how beautiful the islands were."

"They are—in their own way. Here, the colors are more subtle and muted. The scents aren't cloying; they're earthy. Instead of the beat of the ocean, you have the soughing of the wind. The islands are a testament to God's imagination. Your land is a show of His majesty. Being there was like. . . holding a fistful of jewels. Here is like. . .kneeling in God's presence."

Gideon's intense gaze made her laugh uncomfortably. "Oh dear. I've dithered on, haven't I?"

"Not at all." He slipped his arm about her and took away the rifle. Toting it over his shoulder with ease, he still kept his other arm about her waist and headed toward the house. "Those are some of the nicest words I've ever heard."

Being sheltered in his arms is the nicest feeling I've ever had. Miriam fought the urge to snuggle closer and tried to lighten the conversation. "Speaking of words, can you believe little Ginny Mae? All of a sudden, she's started babbling. She's growing up so fast, Gideon! When I got here, she could barely take a few steps, but now she's toddling everywhere and getting into everything."

"She's a handful, all right. I don't know how you understand her, though. Other than Daddy and 'Pieee' for Polly, I can't make sense of anything she says."

"She calls you 'Geee.'"

Gideon snorted. "She's also called every one of my brothers and the barn cat that."

"She spends most of her waking hours with me. Of course I understand what she means."

He halted at once and gave her a piercing look. "I thought you wanted to mind the girls. We men can start—"

"Gideon Chance, don't you dare tromp down that path! My only regret is that I wasn't here to help with Polly when she was younger."

"You sure?"

"You know I adore those little girls! I know you all did your best for them, but they need a woman's touch. It tears me apart, knowing Hannah isn't here to mother them. But you have to know I'll love them with every fiber of my being, and I'll care for them as if they were my very own."

"They're a handful."

"They're a heartful," she countered.

"So you still want to stick around here?"

"I've never been more certain of anything in my life. I wrote a letter to my parents last night, telling them all about Polly and Ginny Mae and what it's like here."

"Did you tell them what you said earlier—about it being majestic?"

She nodded. "I told them when I wake up in the morning, this place often makes me think of the verse, 'Be still, and know that I am God.'" She laughed a bit. "Then I told them the day is so full, I don't do much more thinking until I climb back in bed."

"We can still buy your passage back to the islands."

"And cheat me out of the happiness I've found here? Gideon, you couldn't get me to budge from Reliable if you used a crowbar. I love this place, and I love the people even more. Hannah's daughters are delights."

They rounded the garden and headed toward the main house. Daniel was kneeling in the dirt, brushing off Ginny's dress and face. Polly turned and ran toward Miriam. "Ginny fell, Auntie Miri-Em!"

Ginny wiggled away from Daniel and headed for Miriam, too. Tears streaked her grubby little cheeks as she raised her arms to be lifted. "M'um! M'um!"

"Mom!" Accusation thundered in Dan's voice.

fourteen

Gideon tightened his hold around Miriam as his brother stormed toward her. "Daniel—"

"You stay out of this." Daniel jabbed his forefinger at Miriam. "You taught her that. You had no right. She's not yours."

"Paul. Titus." Gideon did his best to keep his voice level and calm as he summoned his brothers. The last thing he wanted was to have the babies witness this confrontation. Polly's eyes were huge, and Ginny tugged at Miriam's skirts and continued to cry, "M'um! Up!"

Both brothers had been nearby. They closed ranks on either side of him and Miriam.

"The girls." The words barely made it out of his mouth before Paul stooped to sweep the baby and Polly into his arms. "C'mon, girls. Uncle Paul wants to show you a big, fat worm." He strode away.

Titus paused a moment. His chin tilted upward, and he looked from Dan to Miriam, then looked at Gideon and raised his brow. "Do you want me to take Miriam inside, or do you need me to knock some sense into Dan?"

"It's none of your affair—neither of you." Dan bristled. "This is betwixt me and Miriam."

Titus whistled under his breath, accepted the rifle from Gideon, and headed into his cabin.

The air crackled with tension.

God, give me wisdom. It's a hard truth I have to tell. "Daniel," Gideon started.

"I told you to stay out of this," Daniel roared. "It's none of your business."

"I never meant to cause discord." Miriam reached out to him. "Daniel, please understand—"

"No, you understand, Miriam. You are not their mother. You'll never be their mother. Hannah was." He thumped his chest. "*My* Hannah. She bore and suckled them. You're their aunt, and that's all you'll ever be."

"That's more than enough for me," she replied with quiet dignity.

For weeks, Gideon had prayed and kept quiet. He knew he had to speak now. "Your girls are lucky to have their auntie M'um. That's right, Dan—*M'um*. It's a baby's way of saying Miriam. If you weren't so busy wallowing in your self-pity, you would have realized it. We've all let you have your temper fits and tried to understand your grief, but you've gone far over the line."

"Fine. Then I'll take my daughters and leave."

Quickly as her hand flew to cover her mouth, Miriam still didn't quite manage to muffle her cry.

"Go? Okay, Dan." Gideon looked his brother in the eyes and called his bluff, not at all sure it was a bluff. "Let's think it through: Just where would you go? Who's going to look after the girls while you work to earn a living?"

"I'd manage."

"You're kidding no one but yourself. You resent Miriam lavishing her love on the girls, but who else would ever treat them with such care?"

"They have my love."

"That they do. They have mine, too, just as they have Paul, Titus, Logan, and Bryce's love. Taking them away from all of us would be cruel to them, and you know it."

"You've given me no choice. It's either me or her." He gave Miriam a malevolent glare.

Gideon rested his hands on Miriam's shoulders in a silent show of support. "Her name is Miriam, and you'll use it. Polly and Ginny Mae need Miriam. She's become part of this family—an important part, and it's high time you accept that fact."

"I don't expect you to understand."

"All I know is, you're suffering from grief now, but how much more are your daughters going to suffer if they don't grow up with a woman's love? It's not about you. It's about Polly and Virginia." Something flared in Daniel's eyes, and Gideon paused a moment to let his words sink in. *Lord, please help him understand. Don't let this tear our family apart.* Gideon squeezed Miriam, then moved to the side and clamped his hand on Daniel's shoulder. Quietly he said, "It's bad enough that you sorrow. How could you deny your daughters what they need?"

A wounded sound rumbled deep in Daniel's chest. His face contorted with grief as he turned and shuffled away. Minutes later, the sound of an ax rang over and over and over again.

Tears rained down Miriam's wan cheeks. "What should I do?"

Gideon gathered her to his chest. He bowed his head and whispered into her hair, "Keep doing what you've been doing—love the girls and pray, Miriam. Pray a lot."

ॐ

When they'd all been together in the one dwelling, the brothers often urged Miriam to read aloud from her Bible as they wound up an evening. Since the day they'd built all of the cottages, it would have been easy for everyone to just drift off, but they hadn't. Gideon picked up the Bible one night and started reading it aloud. Thereafter, whoever so chose took the honor. By late summer, they'd often go out into the yard, sit together, and hold end-of-the-day devotions.

The resonance in Gideon's voice made the verses seem more special and personal. Miriam didn't want to think about that fact, but as she lay in bed one night, she closed her eyes and heard the middle verses of the first chapter of 2 Timothy as he'd read it that night:

> *"Nevertheless I am not ashamed: for I know whom I have believed, and am persuaded that he is able to keep that which I have committed unto him against that day. Hold fast the form of sound words, which thou hast heard of me, in faith and love which is in Christ Jesus. That good thing which was committed unto thee keep by the Holy Ghost which dwelleth in us."*

Though she'd memorized that passage as a little girl, it felt as if the Lord had wanted her to hear those words again. *I've committed myself to Thee, Lord. Help me to hold fast to the tasks Thou art entrusting to me. Grant me a loving spirit and a vibrant faith so I can let my light shine in this home. Amen.*

Even after she prayed, Miriam felt restless. It would be so nice to simply dump everything into God's hands and sleep with the innocent trust of a baby. Life wasn't that easy. Especially since Daniel's outburst, she'd felt unsettled. Gideon made it clear he felt she belonged here. Titus, Paul, Logan, and Bryce did, too. Polly and Ginny Mae cuddled with her at every opportunity. Her heart told her this was where she wanted and needed to stay, but Daniel's simmering hostility had turned into a painful, purposeful indifference.

Gideon told Daniel he was acting in his own interest instead of what was best for the girls. Am I fooling myself? Am I staying here not just because I love my nieces but because I've let my heart race ahead of my head and ended up falling in love with Gideon?

❧

"Peeky boo!" Ginny Mae went into gales of giggles as Miriam fluffed a shirt from the laundry line over the child, who sat in the big wicker basket.

Gideon leaned against the clothesline and chuckled. "She's liable to chew on that, you know."

Miriam plucked the next shirt off the line. "It's still damp, anyway."

"Why don't you leave it up awhile, then?"

"I have the irons heating. It'll steam dry."

"The whole time we didn't have a woman here, we never once ironed a work shirt. You could skip that chore, and it wouldn't matter one whit."

Miriam shot him a grin. "Strangers knew you were ranchers because your shirts all looked liked cows chewed on them, huh?"

"The finest cows in the state." He puffed out his chest. "We took it as a mark of honor."

He watched as she took a scrap of fabric down from the line and knelt with Polly. Carefully she taught Polly how to wrap up her dolly. Polly's face lit with delight. "Looky, Unca Giddy—looky at my dolly!"

"That's just how your mama used to wrap you." He'd spoken without thinking, but judging from their glowing smiles, Gideon reckoned he'd managed to say the right thing.

Miriam rose and shoved back a damp curl. "Reba said there's a circuit rider coming through, so we'll have a real preacher this week."

"Oh, so we're going to all have to be in our best Sunday-go-to-meeting duds?" He took one end of the sheet off the line and helped her match the corners and fold it. When they met in the middle, he added, "Folks have been right happy with how we've been holding worship on our own."

She tilted her head to the side. "Do you think it's the worship or that we have a meal afterward?"

"Does it matter? Whether they come for the sake of their souls or their bellies, the men are being fed. We're shining light, Miriam."

Her face brightened. "Yes, we are, aren't we?"

"Absolutely." He lifted the laundry basket—Ginny Mae included—and carried it to the main house. "Got word from Chris Roland that he'll be slaughtering a steer tomorrow. He'll bring over a hindquarter so the boys can barbecue it for Sunday."

"That's a blessing." Preceding him into the house, she motioned toward the table.

He set down the laundry and watched as she took two loaves of bread from the oven and slipped in another pair. The yeasty fragrance never ceased to please him. "Mmm-mmm. Think heaven smells that good?"

Miriam laughed. "Oh, I think heaven smells like the cedar trees past the garden—probably because of the verses about the cedars of Lebanon for the temple." She lifted Ginny Mae from the depths of the laundry basket. "Polly, honey, it's nap time."

"I'm not tired." Polly's jaw jutted out.

Gideon knew the look well, and he opened his mouth to scold her, but Miriam's reaction stopped him short. She simply plucked the rag doll from Polly's arms and walked away. Her words drifted over her shoulder. "Well, that's a sad thing.

Dolly and sister are going to be lonely, napping without you."

Polly scrambled into the big, old bedroom. A corner of it now held a little trundle bed and a crib where the girls took their naps. "I want my dolly!"

"Then you need to take off your shoes and get in bed." Miriam kept the doll out of reach and started changing Ginny's diaper.

"Unca Giddy, Auntie Miri-Em is mean. Tell her not to be bad to me."

"Polly, you're being a naughty girl." He wagged his finger at her. "A very naughty girl. You're to mind what Aunt Miriam tells you to do. She loves you and would never be mean to you."

"But she gots Dolly!"

"She's being nice. She said if you take off your shoes and get in bed, you may have Dolly back. Sassy as you've been, I would have swatted your backside and kept Dolly."

"But you're a big growed-up man." Her lower lip started to quiver. "You don't need Dolly to cuddle."

"Miriam made Dolly. That makes Dolly very special, and I'd be happy to mind such a fine toy. Even grown-ups like cuddling."

Little braids swinging from the vehemence with which she shook her head, Polly said, "Nuh-unh. Hugs and cuddles is for babies and little girls."

"Snippy little girls get swats, not hugs." He folded his arms across his chest. "Now get those shoes off and climb into bed."

Miriam kissed Ginny Mae's cheek, laid her in the crib, and covered her. "Night-night."

"Nigh-nigh."

Polly yanked off her shoes, scrambled onto her bed, and thrust out her hands. "Dolly!" She hurriedly tacked on, "Please!"

Miriam knelt by the bed and carefully tucked Dolly in

next to Polly. She dallied for a moment, then cupped Polly's cheek. "Grown-ups who love each other and get married hug, sweetheart."

"Did my daddy and mama hug?"

"Yes. They loved each other very, very much. Now you have a nice nap and hold Dolly tight."

With the girls situated, Miriam and Gideon went back to the main room. Miriam let out a sigh as she checked the sadirons on the stove.

"You're tired. Why don't you rest while the girls nap?"

"It's not that." Tears filled her pretty green eyes. "Polly's never going to have the security of seeing Hannah and Daniel embracing."

"Shh." He tugged her away from the stove. "Remember? That's one of the reasons you need to be here for them—to teach them those little things. You're not just shining God's light, sweet pea, you're shining light to keep the girls from growing up ignorant and backward."

28

The rest of the day passed, and they all gathered outside for Bible reading. Miriam caught Gideon giving her a baffled look, and her cheeks went hot with guilt. She hadn't been paying much attention to what Titus read because Gideon's words kept humming through her mind. He'd not just come to accept her here—he'd admitted she belonged and was fulfilling a special calling.

As they broke up after Paul said a prayer, Bryce said, "Betcha we have us a nice, short, misty rain tonight."

Miriam headed toward her cottage, but Gideon stopped her short. "You all that tired?"

"Not really. I was going to crochet or sew a bit."

The left side of his mouth canted upward. "You've been

sticking close to home. Why don't we just walk a bit?"

Surprised, she allowed him to lead her along the property toward a stand of cedars. "Smells like heaven to me."

"Looks like heaven, too."

Something about his tone made Miriam glance up. Gideon was looking at her—not at the path. *I have to stop this. He's just being a friend. I can't twist his agreement into a compliment. I can't moon over him or make a fool of myself and ruin what we've started.*

"Look to your left," he murmured.

A doe and fawn ventured from behind a tree.

"Polly would enjoy this. If it weren't her bedtime, we could have brought her along." She hoped bringing up the girls would get her mind back where it belonged.

"She'd scare 'em away. She's so noisy, there isn't a creature God made that'll come close to her. Even the dogs keep their distance."

"And I thought Logan wouldn't take her fishing because he was afraid she'd drown!"

"There is that," Gideon agreed. Even in the failing light, she could see the twinkle in his eyes. "Then, too, wherever Polly goes, her baby sister toddles right after. In case it escaped your notice, Ginny Mae seems to enjoy eating the worms instead of leaving them for bait."

Laughter bubbled out of Miriam. For being such a big, brick wall of a man, Gideon Chance hid a well-honed sense of humor and a wellspring of tenderness.

Their conversation and her laughter sent the deer scampering. Miriam let out a sigh. "I didn't stay any quieter than Polly would have."

"I've been seeing deer day in and day out for years; 'til you came, I hadn't heard a woman's laughter in ages."

He led her along a bit farther and paused here and there for her to step over a root or to lift her over a stump. His hands were sure and strong, and when he finally left her at the door to her cabin, Miriam felt bereft as she slid from the shelter of his hold.

"Good night, Gideon. Thank you for the stroll."

"We'll have to do it more often."

"I'd like that." She slipped into her cabin and latched the door. Leaning against the closed door, she listened to him walk off. *Oh, Gideon, I'd really like that.* She thought about getting ready for bed, but the joy of that evening stroll had her wide awake. Sitting on her bed, crocheting, held absolutely no appeal. Miriam decided to slip over into the main house so she could fetch the *Farmer's Almanac*. With the climate here so different, she wanted to study when the best planting time was for various garden crops.

As she headed toward the house, Miriam noted lights still shone in the main room, so she blew out her own candle. No use wasting it. The door stood ajar, and Bryce's hearty chuckle came through. Miriam reached out to push open the door, but she froze when he said, "So she's takin' the bait, huh, Gideon? Imagine that. Drawing straws might not have been the best way to figure out who ought to marry up with her—"

fifteen

Miriam didn't wait to overhear another word. Hand pressed to her mouth, she fled back to her cabin.

Eavesdroppers never hear well of themselves. Mama's oft-times spoken homily taunted Miriam. She hadn't intended to eavesdrop, but she'd definitely gotten an earful. Even in those few seconds, she'd heard more than enough to keep her miserable for the remainder of her days. These barbaric brothers had drawn straws to see who had to wed her? Who were they, to treat her like chattel? Then again, what was so very wrong with her—what did she lack—that not a one of them felt she'd make a suitable mate? They drew straws for her hand—an unwanted bride.

So that's why Gideon's been hanging around the house so much more. Well, no one's going to get stuck with me. I'll refuse his proposal. I won't make a fool of myself, mooning over a man who gets saddled with me because he happened to—

She yanked the pins from her hair and cast them onto the washstand. None of them truly wanted her—not even Gideon. Especially not Gideon.

She grabbed her hairbrush as her hair tumbled in disarray about her shoulders. *He participated in the travesty of drawing straws for my hand?*

Ruthlessly pulling the brush through her hair, Miriam looked at her reflection in the small mirror. *I'm not about to make a fool of myself, mooning over a man who figured he had to be honorable but doesn't really want me. It's better to discover*

Gideon's obligation now rather than to continue to believe a fairy tale I spun for myself. Her hair crackled as the boar bristles raked the full length over and over again.

God, I don't understand why they'd do this. Thou knowest the desires of my heart. Please, Lord, change my heart. Don't let me have feelings for a man who doesn't hold true regard for me.

ℬ

"What happened to Miriam?" Paul whispered the words to Gideon as Miriam took Ginny Mae into the other room for a diaper change.

Gideon winced and shrugged.

"I told you she'd get on our nerves," Daniel rumbled as he shoved away from the table. He cast a look at the doorway and slapped his hat on his head. Ginny Mae was in the middle of a stream of happy-sounding baby babble, and Miriam seemed to be understanding a good portion of it. Daniel turned back for a quick moment, gave Gideon a dark look, then left.

" 'Member when Mama used to get a bee in her bonnet?" Titus leaned forward and swiped the last biscuit. "She'd get this same way."

"What's she got to be riled over?" Logan said. "Gideon's been a regular swain 'round her."

Paul snorted. "That's the problem." Titus and Logan snickered.

"She's not riled." Bryce splashed coffee from the pot over his cup and onto the table. "Why, Miriam is just bein' her usual sweet self." He tossed a dishcloth onto the table and did a slapdash mop-up job.

"Hush." Gideon hoped Miriam wouldn't wonder what all the whispering was about. He raised his voice a bit. "Any more eggs left?"

"Nope. Dan ate the last spoonful." Titus tilted the bowl to prove his point.

Miriam came back into the room with Ginny Mae in her arms. "I'll be happy to scramble more."

"No need." Gideon stood. "Bryce, Roland is bringing part of a steer today. I want you to fix up the barbecue pit. Daniel will bring wood over to you."

Miriam wouldn't look him in the eye, and Gideon couldn't figure out why she acted so. . .different this morning. She'd twisted her hair up same as always and wore one of her old, ugly dresses, so she ought to look the same, but her smile seemed forced as she started to clear the table. "Anyone have something special they'd like me to fix for Sunday supper?"

"Chocolate cake," Bryce voted.

"Pudding, please," Polly requested.

"Since you're asking—" Titus began.

"Hold your horses." Gideon glowered at them. "Miriam's going to fix whatever suits her fancy. She's not here to dance a jig to your tunes."

Miriam turned to carry the dishes to the sink. "It's no problem for me to make what someone might want."

"I do have a hankering for—"

Gideon silenced Titus with a look. "I'm sure whatever Miriam makes will be delicious. We need to get to work."

"Paul? Could you please bring me your blue shirt? I noticed it needs to be mended." Miriam dipped hot water from the stove reservoir to use for dishwashing.

By supper, a platter heaped with steaming chicken-fried steaks drew the men to the table. Gideon frowned at the empty place beside him. "Come eat, Miriam."

"Oh, I already ate an early supper with the girls." She busied herself, pumping water into a pail.

"What are you doing?"

"Saturday bath water, right?" Paul guessed.

"Yes." She flashed a smile over her shoulder.

Gideon pushed away from the table and stalked across the kitchen. He hefted the bucket of water and thumped it onto the stove, then filled another pail and placed it on the stove, as well. "Ask for help with that, Miriam. It's too heavy for you."

"Nonsense." She dried her hands off on the hem of her apron and headed toward the other room. "Come along, my little poppets." Polly scampered in her wake, and Ginny followed with the eager, flat-footed patter only a baby in a full diaper could manage.

Splashes and giggles from the bedroom made it clear the girls enjoyed bath time. Gideon still scowled at his full plate. Somehow, with Miriam absent, the meal didn't appeal to him half as much. When the splashing ended, he fully expected Miriam to reappear.

He was wrong.

"Hey." Logan elbowed him. "I asked for the applesauce."

"Oh. Here." Gideon shoved the bowl into his brother's hands. The meal was over before Miriam and the girls reappeared. Both girls wore nightgowns Miriam had made from feed sacks that bore little bitty chickens all over them. Ginny Mae's baby curls fluffed out like duck down.

"Lookit me!" Polly twirled around.

"What happened to your head?" Bryce squinted at her.

"Auntie Miri-Em stuck rags in my hair. I'm going to have pretty curls."

"I'll tuck them in bed if you'd like to take your bath now, Daniel." Miriam stooped down to fuss with Ginny's sleeve.

"No. I tuck my girls in." Daniel cast a glance at his brothers. "They can keep an eye on my daughters for me."

"Not 'til after you do supper dishes." Titus plopped down on the floor and tickled under Polly's chin. "It's your turn to dry the dishes, Dan. I'm washin' tonight."

"Dishes are a woman's job," Dan gritted.

"You didn't say that when Hannah was here." Paul's words made everything in the room go still. "We all pitched in and did dishes back then."

"Miriam's done plenty enough already." Gideon stared at Daniel. "She's washed and ironed everyone's clothes for church tomorrow. She's cooked and cleaned, gardened, and minded your children."

"Mended my shirt, too," Paul added.

The door clicked shut. Gideon wheeled around and discovered Miriam had slipped out.

❧

"Miriam, this is Dr. Pendergast." Reba White fluttered her fan with skill any Southern belle would admire. "Dr. Pendergast, may I present you to Miss Miriam Hancock."

The doctor swept off his gray bowler and bowed quite elegantly. "A pleasure, Miss Hancock."

Miriam watched him straighten up and wondered why a man of such noble and lucrative profession would be attired in such ill-fitting clothes. She'd been reared not to judge a man by his appearance, but something didn't strike her as being right.

"I'm pleased to have an opportunity to speak with a physician. With the girls so small, and—"

"Oh no. That's not it at all." Reba giggled. "He's a phrenologist, dear. I told him he simply must examine your head to be sure that bump you received upon your arrival didn't cause you any harm."

"I've worried 'bout that," Logan confessed. "I didn't mean

to brain you, Miriam. You know I didn't."

"I'm fine. Truly I am."

"It would be wise to have a professional ascertain that." Dr. Pendergast started to remove his dove gray gloves.

"I don't—"

"It won't take much time, and it won't hurt at all."

"How much does it cost?" Bryce stuck his hand into his pocket. To Miriam's consternation, he pulled out half a dozen screws and nails. He pursed his lips and shook his head. "Heard the jingle. Forgot it wasn't cash money."

"Bryce, please don't put those back into your Sunday-best pants. They'll ruin the pocket."

He'd already started. As a nail hit the earth by his boot, a sheepish look crossed his face. "Oops. Too late."

"It's not a problem, young man. I can tell from here. See?" The phrenologist ran his fingers over the back of her head. "This is the area denoting domesticity. Miss Hancock is endowed with a veritable ridge in this location."

"Uh-oh." Logan's face turned an odd combination of green and purple. "Does that mean when I brained her, it broke her head?"

"That has yet to be ascertained. Come, now, Miss Hancock. It's far better if you sit for your reading."

"Yes, Miriam. You must!" Reba half dragged her to a chair.

Before she knew what happened, Miriam was sitting on a bench and had her hair streaming down her shoulders and back. Dr. Pendergast's fingers skated over her scalp. She shivered and tried to pull away. "I must insist you cease this." Miriam wiggled. "Logan, I don't believe in this. It's a dark art, and I won't be a part of it."

"Young lady, this is medical science." Dr. Pendergast kept his palm atop her head and continued to slip the fingertips of his other hand along her head. "The apostle Luke was a physician."

"A physician, not a phrenologist!"

"Ah, you're displaying remarkable stubbornness—which is confirmed here, by this region of the brow."

"She can be a mite stubborn," Bryce allowed.

"I'm going to be more than a little stubborn if you don't turn loose of me."

"Women are wont to be emotional. Here, the prominence over the seat of emotions tells me she's often overwrought. My, my. Here, over the area of spiritual enlightenment—an area of concavity."

"That's about where she got the lump when Logan brained her." Bryce leaned forward.

"Concavity means it dips in, not lumps out." Miriam wrenched loose. "Sir, to pretend education, discipline, and salvation cannot overcome natural formations of the skull is heresy. I—"

"What is going on here?" Gideon shoved through the knot of men who had congregated and pressed in around her. His eyes widened as he caught sight of her with her hair in disarray.

"We was just trying to be sure the doc got a chance to make sure Miriam's in her right mind." Three more screws clinked on the ground by Bryce's foot.

"A doctor? Good. It would be better if you did this inside."

"He's a quack, Gideon." Miriam tried to twist her hair back into a decent arrangement but had no way of making it stay since the doctor had done something with her hairpins.

"She's overwrought and stubborn, just as I determined," Pendergast pronounced in a stentorian voice. The men about them nodded and murmured agreement.

Gideon tucked her by his side. Miriam dared hope he'd see

reason, but her hopes disappeared the moment he started walking her toward the house. "It'll only take a few minutes, and it'll make me feel better to know you're all right."

Pendergast trotted on their heels. Gideon didn't just seat her. He kept hold and sat on a bench, dragging her along without any hope of escape. Pendergast kept his opinions to himself and made important-sounding *hmm* and *ahh* sounds as he wiggled his fingers across her head.

Miriam shuddered. "Gideon—"

"It's okay, sweet pea. He'll be done soon. You don't have to be scared." Gideon looked up. "Well, Doc? What do you think?"

"For being a woman, she has reasonable intellect and strong domestic swayings. Science never lies, and it's plain as can be she's spiritually lacking and a woman of dubious virtue. I—"

Gideon let out a roar and bolted to his feet. "You ought to get your head examined if you think that opinion holds any weight here. You're no doctor; you're a charlatan."

"You owe me fifteen cents for my services."

Gideon tucked Miriam behind himself. "You're conducting business on the Lord's Day?"

"Well, sir, the laborer is worthy of his hire."

Paul stood in the open doorway. "Gideon, the men are hungry. When's Miriam going to serve up lunch?"

"As soon as this charlatan stops insulting and swindling her."

Miriam watched as half a dozen men stormed through the house and carried Mr. Pendergast away. Gideon tilted her face up to his. "Well," she said brightly, hoping to evade more than just a second of eye contact, "that's over now."

"He needed to get his own head examined, Miriam. You're the sweetest, most special woman any fellow could ever meet."

She forced a laugh and pulled free. "That settles that. If

ever a real doctor comes by, he'll need to check you because you're definitely not in your right mind!"

❧

Nothing is going right. Nothing. Miriam let out a sigh and decided to take a walk as the girls napped.

Since she'd learned about the brothers drawing straws, everything had seemed to fall apart. Sunday, the so-called doctor declared her to be a woman of no virtue. Monday, she'd burned what should have been a tender roast. Yesterday, the ammonia she wanted to use to wash windows spilled and left the main house reeking. Today, Ginny Mae bit Polly's arm, and Polly whacked her little sister back hard enough to leave a mark on her cheek. Getting both of them settled down for a nap drained the last drop of Miriam's patience.

The cedars beckoned her. Their scent would be a treat, and Miriam needed to indulge herself. She grabbed a pail and walked along the same path Gideon had led her along when they took that stroll—just before she'd learned the truth. Unhappy with that realization, Miriam sidestepped and wandered off a few yards and sauntered along a route of her own choosing.

Sunlight slashed in dusty beams from the treetops. The scent of cedar and pine filled the air. Beneath her feet, pine needles crunched and twigs snapped. Miriam's steps lagged. She'd pick up an occasional pinecone to use as a fire starter for her cottage's potbelly stove.

It felt good to have a few minutes to herself. What once had been a comfortable, happy arrangement now felt strained. Monitoring each word she spoke, each casual touch or glance so they wouldn't carry a hint of interest or flirtation—that drained her.

Miriam knelt to harvest dandelion leaves—one of the few

things around the ranch she knew were edible. *I'm like these. I'm hearty. I can thrive here.* She plucked a top that had gone to seed and upended it to reseed the patch. *I'm not going to blow away. I'm setting down new roots here.*

As she walked, she kept the cabins in sight. She couldn't be gone for long. Again, she crossed the path she and Gideon walked. Her heart twisted. A noble man, he was willing to marry though he felt no *tendre* for her. *Why, God? Why would these feelings for a man fill my heart when all he feels toward me is fraternal concern and obligation? How am I to deal with this?*

After picking more dandelion greens, Miriam headed back toward the house. As she passed the spot under a cedar where she and Gideon had paused to talk on their stroll, she couldn't resist. Miriam picked some wildflowers and an armful of pretty leaves to put in her cottage. They would be a reminder to herself that she could find beauty and pleasure here—even as a spinster.

Miriam left the bucket by the pump in the yard and peeked in to make sure the girls were still napping. Peacefully slumbering as they were, she decided to prop open the door so she could hear them, then went to the garden to do some work.

Awhile later, Daniel startled her out of her musings by striding through the rows of vegetables. "How dim-witted can you be?"

She blinked up at him. "I beg your pardon?"

"The bucket by the pump is your doing, right?"

"Yes. Why?"

"It's full of poison oak." He jabbed a finger toward the bucket. "Go get rid of it and change before you get near my daughters. If your clothes brush them, they'll get the rash. I won't have you harming them."

"Daniel, I'd never knowingly hurt Polly or Virginia." She

headed toward the pump to dispose of the leaves.

"Dump it far away," he called. "The last thing we need is you planting that stuff close by."

By the time she got back, Miriam knew she'd gotten herself into a peck of trouble. Her hands, wrists, and face all started to itch and tingle. At first, she told herself it was just her imagination, but the feeling grew worse.

Daniel sat in the doorway to the main house, using a whetstone to sharpen knives. He didn't even bother to glance up. "Go change your gown. It has to be boiled, else it'll make my girls get the rash."

She got into her cabin, shed her dress, and looked at herself with dismay. Hairline to throat, wrists to fingertips, she was covered in a fine red rash that felt fiery as could be. The cool water from her pitcher didn't help—if anything, it made the itch intensify. Afraid her stockings or petticoat might also carry the rash, she changed every last garment before going back to care for the girls.

Polly hunkered down beside Daniel on the porch, chattering like a magpie. She looked up, and her eyes widened. "Auntie Miri-Em, you is funny!"

A lady does not scratch. Miriam clasped her hands in front of herself to resist the nearly overwhelming urge to abandon her manners. "Yes. I do look odd."

"Go back to your cabin." Daniel concentrated on the edge of the knife he continued to slide along the whetstone. "We can manage just fine without you."

She didn't want to admit defeat, but Miriam couldn't stand the horrid itch much longer. She slipped back into her cottage and cried.

Hours passed, and she thought about making supper. Standing by the hot stove would amount to pure torture.

Nonetheless, the girls and men would need to eat. Perhaps she could make sandwiches just this once. . . .

A single, solid *thump* on her door sounded. "Miriam. Open up."

Gideon. *Of all the people in the world, he's the one I least want to see.* She cleared her throat. "No."

"Dan's minding the girls. Something's up."

"It's nothing."

"If it's nothing, then come on out here." She could hear his boots scuffle in the dirt. "I want to show you something."

"It'll have to wait."

"I'm not going to shout through this door anymore. Now get yourself out here."

"I'm not one of your kid brothers, Gideon. You cannot order me around."

"Hey, Gid!" Logan's voice interrupted their odd disagreement. She ardently hoped Logan would draw him away.

"What?" Already irked, Gideon's voice carried a distinct edge.

"Is Miriam gonna be okay? Dan said she got it bad."

"Got what?"

"Oh. I thought you knew. Dan said—"

Unwilling to be spoken about and well aware the secret was out, she yanked open the door and snapped, "I was an idiot. There. Now leave me alone."

sixteen

Gideon whistled under his breath. Red blazed across Miriam's face, but it owed more to rash than embarrassment. He studied her face, her throat, and looked down at her hands. She'd kept them clasped behind her back, and he suspected she wanted to hide the full extent of her exposure.

"Aw, sweet pea. You tangled with poison oak, didn't you?"

"So Daniel said. I had no notion what it was."

He heaved a sigh. "It's wild. Grows all over."

"And you never mentioned it to me?"

If glares could kill, Gideon reckoned he'd be pushing up daisies about now. "I'll go fetch some milk and churn it. Mama used buttermilk on us whenever we—"

"I'll churn my own buttermilk."

"No." He pointed at the bed. "You go have a rest. The salt from sweat only makes the rash itch worse."

She gave him a horrified look. "Are you implying I sweat, Gideon Chance?"

He had the sinking feeling whatever he said, it would only make matters worse. He opted for escape. "I'll be back. Leave your door open so your cottage has lots of fresh air—"

"So I won't sweat?"

Figuring he'd be signing his own death warrant no matter what he said, Gideon left. Her door was shut when he returned, and he couldn't help chuckling. Feisty as could be, Miriam wasn't about to show any weakness, and this wasn't really anything more than a bout of misery. He drummed his fingers on her windowpane.

The yellow curtain swished to the side, and a slate appeared. "Leave me be," he read aloud.

The slate disappeared as the curtain swished back down.

"All right, Miriam. I'll leave you be. . ." He paused, then tacked on, "u-t-t-e-r-m-i-l—"

The door opened. "You are a nuisance, Gideon." The fire in her green eyes turned into a twinkle. "And a terrible guide. I'm holding you responsible for this tragedy."

"You couldn't have gotten this from where we went on our stroll. I know for a fact that path's clear as can be."

"You should have made sure nothing poisonous was around the property, and you certainly could have warned me about it."

"We try to keep it hacked back, but you must have gone off the path." Her mouth opened in a perfect O that could have denoted either shock or guilt, but Gideon didn't want either, so he hastily added, "Truth is, no one's sure exactly how many variations there are of the pesky stuff."

Her speckled brow creased. "Then how do you avoid it?"

He stuck his bandanna into the gloppy buttermilk and dabbed it on her cheek. "You do your best. Other than staying where things are cleared, just remember a saying: 'Leaves of three, let them be.' It seems many of the varieties of poison oak bear three leaves to the stem."

"Now you tell me," she muttered. He nudged her chin with his thumb so he could get to her throat, but she resisted and claimed, "I can take care of myself. Just tell me how long I'm going to itch."

"Can't say." He refused to stop. Dipping the bandanna back into the buttermilk, he recalled, "My last episode lasted about six days. I have water in the wash kettle comin' to a boil so we can dunk your dress."

"If that works with the clothes, why wouldn't a hot bath take away my rash?"

"Because that would make life too easy." He daubed her nose. "Life out here is never easy."

≈

Miriam had been trying to find things to occupy her time since Gideon decreed she wasn't allowed to do anything for the next week. Dreadfully as she itched and as horrid as the rash looked, she didn't exactly mind that order the first two days. In fact, adding a cup of baking soda to the big galvanized tub was the only time she got any respite.

Gideon brought over the green paisley material and the lace he'd bought in town for her. Her hands hurt, but she stitched on the dress so she wouldn't be tempted to scratch.

"Miriam?" Paul leaned against her doorjamb. "Got any good ideas on what to make for supper?"

"What about some corn chowder?" She gave him explicit instructions and fully expected to have him return to review them a time or two. Judging from the food the men had been fixing the last few days, Miriam decided their survival bordered on the miraculous. No matter what the dish, they managed to botch it somehow or another.

She sat at the little drop-leaf desk in her cottage and finished writing another letter to her cousin. Delilah had managed to send her a note last week, and Miriam invited her to come for a visit whenever she'd like to. *It shouldn't cause a problem if she accepts. Delilah can stay here in my cottage with me.*

After she pasted shut the envelope, Miriam looked out her open door and waited until she spied the next Chance to pass by. "Titus?"

"Yep?"

"I'd like to post a letter. Could you please help me hitch up the buckboard? I'll take the girls to town with me."

He shook his head. "Nope. Gideon said you're off work detail until Monday. 'Sides, I just got back from town. Brought back more baking soda for you to soak in."

"How thoughtful. That terrible itch is almost gone now, but it's good to have a supply on hand, just in case."

Titus scuffed his boot in the dirt. "Truth is, I was hoping maybe I could talk with you a minute or so."

"Sure." She left her cottage and sat out on a bench. Titus ambled alongside her, but he didn't take a seat. Instead, he planted one boot on the bench beside her and leaned forward so he could lean on that knee.

"Something's on your mind, Titus?"

He nodded. "A gal."

"Hmm."

"She's as purty as a speckled pup, Miriam—only she'd have a hissy fit if she heard me say such a thing. She's cultured and classy—went to a finishing school."

"Oh, the Whites' daughter is back?"

"That's the one." A slow smile lit his face. The expression made him look even more like Gideon than usual. "She came in on the stage today. You've never seen such a day gown. I venture she has more rows of ribbons and lace on it than—" He stopped abruptly and went ruddy.

"So she has lovely clothes." Miriam ignored whatever avenue his mind might have been traveling and pulled him back to the subject. "Did you invite her to attend church?"

"Her mama already said they were a-comin'."

"Then you'll have to maneuver so as to be seated next to the lovely lady."

"Now that's a dandy plan." Titus leaned closer and lowered his voice. "Priscilla just got back, but a fellow can't wait—not around here. I'm figuring maybe I ought to pop the question straightaway, before some other buck does, so I have dibs on her."

"Titus! Were you and Miss White courting before she left, or did you have an understanding?"

"No." His expression turned guarded.

"How can you know if she's the right one, then? She may be a vision of beauty, but that doesn't mean the Lord intends your souls to be forged into one. It's not the outward appearance that should count. You're worth more than having a china doll on your arm, Titus. You deserve a woman who will be your helpmeet and share her heart with you."

"I could ask Paul to move in with Gideon so I'd be able to offer her a place of our own. I'd even be willing to go into town to help her pa at the store if he needs me."

"You're willing to offer your goods and your muscles, Titus. That's a start. But are you willing to share your heart? Do you even know if Priscilla has any feelings for you? Working hard and being attracted are fine, but they aren't enough to make a marriage work."

"I just don't want someone else to beat me to the punch and snap her up. We don't get many womenfolk up here."

"You asked my opinion, and from a woman's perspective, I have to tell you that a man who wants a bride based only on her availability or appearance isn't the kind of man a worthy woman would wed." She reached over and touched his arm. "Pray before you act."

"Can't say I'm surprised you said that, but ever notice that fellas move a lot faster than God lots of the time?"

"You're right. Maybe that's why the world is in such a state."

Titus wandered off to do some praying and thinking. Miriam sat on the bench and closed her eyes. She needed to listen to her own advice. A man who wanted a woman just because she was available ought never propose. She wouldn't put up with such a sham marriage. *Gideon might have drawn the short straw, but that doesn't mean I have to accept if he proposes. He can just go search for a bride elsewhere.*

❧

"Now that was a fine meal. Don't know how you do it, but every last thing you make is a treat." Gideon smiled at Miriam as he pulled her chair back from the supper table. She'd made a zesty chili and corn bread and topped off the meal with a fine-tasting berry pie. Far as he was concerned, life didn't get better than that.

"Thank you. I'm glad you liked it." She rose and began stacking dishes.

He reached over and took the plates from her and set them back down on the table. "How about going for a stroll?"

"I'd rather not."

Her refusal surprised him. He steered her out to the porch as his brothers started to clear the table and squabble over who was supposed to wash dishes. Gideon turned her and held both arms above the elbows to be sure he wasn't bothering any last splotches of her poison oak rash. Studying her eyes, he wondered aloud, "You're not still sore at me about forgetting to tell you about the poison oak, are you?"

"I've forgiven you."

He couldn't resist smiling back at her. Sweetness radiated from the woman. Trailing his fingers down her soft cheek, he rumbled, "If you're afraid I'll walk you through a patch, I'll carry a lantern."

Miriam shied away from his touch. "There are better ways to shine your light."

He chuckled at her cleverness, but he still hadn't succeeded in his goal. He wanted to be alone with her. "Tell you what. Come with me to shut the chickens back into the coop."

"Okay. Did you know two of the eggs this morning were double yolked?"

Most of the hens were content to get back to their nests as twilight fell. A few stubborn ones scattered and needed to be chased down. Once done with that task, Gideon shut one large door of the chicken "cabinet" as Miriam shut the other. He met her in the middle and latched it closed.

"We make a good team." He silently congratulated himself on that segue. Surely it counted as a slick way to ease into an opportunity to pop the question.

"I've been impressed by the way you and your brothers work together to keep this place going."

"That's a mighty fine compliment." He smiled at her. "Your opinion holds a lot of sway with me, so that makes your words count for even more."

Miriam looked as if she were ready to head toward her cottage, and Gideon slipped a hand around her wrist to hold her back. Now that he'd screwed up the courage, he wanted to get this over with.

"Miriam, you're already part of the family, but I'd like to make it formal. Will you do me the honor of becoming my wife?"

seventeen

Your offer is generous, but I'm afraid I'll have to decline."

Gideon stared at Miriam in disbelief. He'd never imagined she'd refuse his proposal. It was all supposed to be so easy, so practical. Miriam never stirred up problems; she solved them. What had gotten into her, to wreck his carefully laid plans?

"Why not?" He blurted out the question.

Even in the evening light, he could see the color drain from her face. "It's not right," she stammered. "It just won't work."

"But—"

"Please excuse me. . . ." She dashed back to her cottage and shut the door so fast, a stranger would have thought the hounds of Hades were on her heels.

Gideon beat his hat against his thigh and headed toward the barn. He needed time alone. Never had it occurred to him that Miriam wouldn't consider the two of them to be a suitable match. At the moment, he had to figure out what to do next.

Unfortunately, Paul was in the barn. He folded his arms on the top of a stall door. "Well, when's the big day?"

"It isn't."

"Oh. You sure are takin' your time at all of this courtin' business. I thought for sure you were trying to get Miriam to go for a walk so's you could propose."

"I asked; she refused." The admission stung his pride, but the hurt went far deeper than that. Gideon couldn't figure out why.

"What did you do wrong?"

What did I do wrong? The question kept running through

155

Gideon's mind. A proposal in front of a chicken coop wasn't exactly romantic enough to make a girl swoon with delight, but Miriam wasn't like other gals. Besides, he'd tried to get her to take a walk. She just didn't cooperate.

"Did you think to show her Ma's ring so she knew you weren't funnin' her?"

"I'm not bribing a woman to be my bride!"

Paul heaved a sigh. "I didn't say you were. I reckoned since she turned you down, maybe she took it for a joke—like she did the day we built the cabins. She didn't realize Marv was making a serious offer. Could be, the gal just didn't understand you meant business."

"Mind your own business, Paul." *She had to know I was serious. Maybe I just shocked her. She might need time getting used to the notion.*

"Fine. She's your problem."

"She's not a problem; she's just confused. Women sometimes need to let an idea take root."

"Yeah. Ma was like that. Said she liked to sleep on things." Paul shrugged. "If it doesn't work out, Titus and I'll go ahead and draw straws."

Gideon glowered, and Paul left the barn. Gideon paced back and forth, trying to determine what had made calm, meek Miriam run off. *Maybe she thinks it's wrong to have a wedding since Hannah died. But Hannah died nearly a year ago. Silly woman scampered off too fast. I need to reason with her.*

❧

Heart breaking asunder, Miriam curled up on her bed. Gideon had offered her what she most wanted, but it would be an empty marriage because he felt no love for her. *God, please help me. Strengthen me. Make this terrible situation go away. I can't bear to see Gideon again tomorrow. I don't know what to do.*

She'd come to her cabin because she couldn't bear to have Gideon offer matrimony when his heart wasn't in it. Her refusal was supposed to free him of any obligation.

A man who loves a woman pursues her, courts her, woos her. I won't bind him to me because he has misguided loyalties to his brothers and nieces. Someday, when he meets the woman of his dreams, he'll thank me for letting him off the hook. The idea of Gideon falling in love and marrying someone else made her bury her face in the pillow and start crying again.

Papa always spoke the message, but Mama had a knack for speaking words of wisdom at the right time. Miriam wished Mama were here to share this burden. *I rely on God's Word and prayer, but when I flounder, God sometimes speaks to me in a song.* Mama's words sifted through Miriam's aching heart. She huddled on the bed and waited. Soon a hymn threaded through her mind.

When darkness seems to hide His face, I rest on His unchanging grace. The lyrics pulled at her. She started to hum but gave up. All she managed was a broken, off-key croak—a pathetic sound that matched the shattered feeling in her heart. *When all around my soul gives way, He then is all my Hope and Stay.*

Miriam wiped tears from her face. *Lord, be my Hope and Stay. Everything around me is giving way, but Thou changest not.*

In the midst of her prayer, a solid, single *thump* rattled her door. Gideon. No one else "knocked" like that.

"Miriam!"

No one else bellowed like that, either.

"We need to talk."

She sat on the edge of her bed. "You're not talking; you're hollering like a madman."

"If I'm insane, it's your fault." He lowered his voice. "Take pity on me and get out here."

"Why don't you take pity on me and leave me alone?"

He groaned. "You've been crying, haven't you?"

She didn't answer. Lying was a sin, but she figured keeping her mouth shut wasn't exactly the same thing. He didn't have a right to know how she felt anyway.

"We can work this out. I know we can," he cajoled.

Waiting wasn't going to make the problem go away. If anything, the longer Gideon stood out there, talking at her door, the greater the chances were that all of his brothers would get involved in this travesty. Miriam crossed the floor.

"Any problem can be worked out if folks are reasonable."

"And," she said as she opened the door and stared up into his face, "they have a handful of straws."

Gideon gave her a baffled look.

Mortified to the core, Miriam admitted, "I know about what happened. You're supposed to be stuck with me, but I'm not going to be a part of it. So now can we stop all of this embarrassing nonsense and get back to being normal?"

"If you knew, why are you mad?"

"You mean, you're supposed to have that right because you're the one who lost and drew the short straw?" Her jaw jutted out. "You can be a happy man again. Go back and tell your brothers I let you off the hook."

"Have you taken leave of your senses? Why would I do an idiotic thing like that?"

Miriam let out a choppy sigh. "I'm not going to run away with some other rancher or cowboy. I'm committed to staying here."

"That's all well and good, but—"

"So you didn't have to draw straws. It was unnecessary."

"Sweet pea, I don't get it at all. If anything, I'd think you'd feel better, knowing how that all worked out."

She stared at him in utter amazement.

Gideon's expression shifted. "Bryce is the only one who would have blabbed. What did he tell you?"

"I refuse to discuss this."

"Tough. I want you for my bride. I refused to take a chance at not having you. My mama and daddy were a love match, and I wouldn't settle for anything less. You're my one-in-a-million chance to truly be happy, and I want to make you happy, too. I couldn't risk Paul or Titus getting the straw, so I took 'em all."

"*What?*"

"Right out there in the barn in front of my brothers, I grabbed those straws and ground them into the dust." He let out a rueful chuckle at the memory. "Titus teased me about volunteering, and I shocked him out of his socks when I said I couldn't stand to let you go to anyone else—that you were mine." He spread his hands. "If you're wanting fancy courtin', I'll do my dead-level best, but I'm warning you here and now, I'm liable to make a mess of it."

"Yup, he is," Bryce called.

"Hush and get in the house." Gideon didn't even bother to look over his shoulder. He continued to look her in the eyes. "I've got me five pesky brothers and a busy ranch, but that's just the world God set me in. It wasn't 'til the day you arrived that I came to life. You challenged me to be the man God wants me to be. You brightened each day."

"You feel that way about me?"

"Sweet pea, you marched in here and stole my heart before I knew what happened. I love you. Now I was hopin' to take you on a nice stroll under the moon and declare my undying love, but you're skittish of poison ivy. Where's a fellow to take his gal so's he can propose?"

She stood on tiptoe and whispered in his ear, "You can take me in your arms, Gideon. That's where I'd really love to be."

⁂

Two weeks later, Gideon and Paul rode out to check on fencing. Titus went to town, and Gideon suspected he'd be there awhile. He'd nicked himself shaving, borrowed Paul's bay rum, and gladly accepted Miriam's offer to iron his shirt.

"Titus is sweet on Priscilla White," Paul said.

"I figured as much. A man's got a right to pick his mate. Can't say I'd be thrilled if he marries her, though." Gideon eased back in the saddle. "Her pa calls her 'Prissy' for good cause."

"Her mama wants her to catch the banker. Rovel has more money than anyone else hereabouts. Expensive as all of Priscilla's dresses are, I reckon she'll want a man with wads of money."

"Don't tell Titus that. He'll figure it out soon enough."

Not long thereafter, Titus rode up. He took off his hat and wiped the sweat from his brow with his sleeve. "You're never gonna believe this."

"What I believe is, you'd best better use your bandanna instead of your sleeve." Gideon scowled at him. "Miriam's already busy enough without having to do extra laundry."

"That's what I'm talking about."

"Laundry?"

"No. Miriam being busy. She's not going to be in the least bit happy, Gideon. It's going to upset her."

"What's going to upset her?"

"I saw the circuit rider."

Gideon's eyes narrowed. "Where? When?"

"He stopped through here to announce he's takin' on a regular pastorate and won't be coming through anymore."

"Not yet, he can't! The wedding's in two weeks."

Titus slapped his hat back on his head. "Well, that's why I'm here—to tell you that he'll come out to the house at breakfast tomorrow to do the wedding. It's either that, or you and Miriam will have to go into San Francisco alone to get hitched properlike."

Gideon turned his horse toward the house. During the half hour it took to ride there, he tried to figure out how to break the news to Miriam. From the evening she'd accepted his proposal, she'd been working on plans for a storybook wedding. Every evening, she'd chatter on about what she'd done that day. A whole hive of bees couldn't come close to matching such industry. Their honey wouldn't be half as sweet, either.

A newly made wedding shirt awaited Gideon. Miriam had sent all of the brothers out with fancy handwritten invitations. She'd gotten Paul to build an altar and Bryce to polish Mama's silver candlesticks. By transplanting clumps of wildflowers, she had the yard looking downright fancy. Come winter, those flowers would die out, but he didn't have the heart to tell her so. As long as she was happy and they'd make for her fairy-tale-perfect wedding, everything suited him just fine.

The problem was, if they got married tomorrow, she wouldn't have the fancy cake all baked or her dress finished. She thought she had fourteen days; she had fourteen hours.

eighteen

Hitching Splotch outside the house, Gideon rehearsed what he'd say. Reba White stood in the door like an avenging angel and made him lose his lines when she dramatically struck a pose very much like a starfish holding fast to the doorjamb and squawked, "Get back on your horse this very minute! You're not allowed here."

"I need to see Miriam."

"Absolutely not!"

Gideon headed for the door, fully expecting Reba to calm down and yield. "Reba, this is important."

She looked as belligerent as a just-saddled feral mustang. "Nothing is more important than your future."

"Yup. That's why I need to see Miriam." He stepped forward, figuring Reba would cave in and back up so he'd get by her. He was wrong. Toe-to-toe with her, he glared down. "I don't have time to waste here."

"You've got a lifetime, cowboy. Whatever you have to say can just wait 'til supper." She whispered, "We're working on Miriam's dress. You can't see it."

"I don't care about the dress; it's Miriam I need to see."

"She's in it—or what we have started of it. I have her pinned into the bodice, and it's taken us all morning to get it just right."

"Good. So it's done." That boded well. Relief flooded him.

"Done?" Reba laughed. "Gideon, it's just pinned. We have to sew it together and—"

"Miriam." He raised the volume slightly without letting the dread show. His bride set lots of store in having this pretty dress, and he was going to have to tell her—

"Yes?"

"Come here, sweet pea." Rustling told him she'd be there in a minute.

Wrapped in the tablecloth, she appeared just behind Reba. An area about the size of his fist got singed on the tablecloth when he'd wrapped her in it to extinguish the fire. He didn't tell Miriam he could see airy white material through the hole. She'd already listed crocheting a tablecloth as something she needed to do before the wedding. *One more reason for her to get in a dither.*

Reba waggled her finger under his nose. "No peeking." She scuttled into the other room to give them some privacy.

"You're beautiful." The words slipped out of his mouth, and Miriam's smile was ample reward. *Lord, let it all go this well.*

"It's taken hours, but we have the design all set, Gideon. I want my gown to be beautiful for you—and for our daughter to wear on her wedding day."

"That's what I have to tell you—our wedding day. It's tomorrow."

Merry laughter bubbled out of her. When he didn't join in, her laughter died out. Her eyes grew huge.

"The circuit rider will be here in the morning. He's taken a regular pastorate, so he's not available for our original date." There. He'd said the lines he'd planned, and he'd gotten them out quite smoothly.

"We'll just have to wait for the next circuit rider, then."

"We are not waiting." He gave her the glower that always made his kid brothers toe the mark. "It took us two years before we got that parson. There's no telling how long it'll take before we'll have another man of the cloth to officiate. We're getting married tomorrow."

"But that was before this area became civilized and so well populated, Gideon." Completely unaffected by his glower, she gave him her I'm-being-practical smile. "We're bound to have a parson arrive in a matter of months."

"Months!"

She bobbed her head, and her eyes brightened. "Why, it's actually a blessing, Gideon. It'll give me more time on my gown, and—"

"We're getting married in the morning, Miriam. I don't care if you're in your nightdress or Bryce's britches. You'll be my bride tomorrow." Her face went pale as he thundered those words, and Gideon wished he'd been more diplomatic. "Swathed in a tablecloth, you're beautiful, Miriam. I couldn't care less about what you're wearing. I just want you to be mine."

She held the tablecloth tightly about herself and squared her shoulders. Moments passed, and several expressions flitted across her face. Her voice quavered. "You're marrying me, not my dress. I understand. A sound marriage is more important than an elaborate wedding."

"We can still celebrate in two weeks—make that date a fancy reception." There. That qualified as a good compromise.

Miriam nodded slowly.

He trailed his fingers down her cheek. She'd lost her sparkle, and he knew he'd just destroyed her plans for a dreams-come-true wedding. "I'm sorry it worked out this way. You had it all planned out. Our only other choice would be to go to San Francisco and get married there."

"Would everybody come with us?" Hope flickered in her eyes.

"No. Too much to be done around here."

"I don't want to go off and get married among strangers. A wedding is all about love and family."

Reba called out softly, "I don't mean to be rude, but time's a-wasting, and these girls are going to wake up from their nap soon."

"Come on out," Gideon said. "Maybe you and Miriam can fix something she can wear. Things got moved up. The wedding's in the morning."

Reba gave a yelp. "Tomorrow!" She gave Gideon an outraged look. "Impossible. She doesn't have a dress. The netting I ordered for her veil isn't even here yet!"

Why did women put store by such silly fripperies? But Gideon saw the wince Miriam hadn't managed to hide at the mention of a veil. He could solve that problem. "Veils are wretched things. A man ought to have the pleasure of seeing his bride's radiance. Given my druthers, I want flowers in her hair."

"Well, now, there's a fine plan." Reba perked up.

Miriam managed a wobbly smile. "I used up all the eggs this morning. Could you go rustle up a few more? I'll need them for the cake."

"Cake?"

Her brow arched. "You don't think we're getting married without a wedding cake, do you?"

Laughter bellowed out of him. She'd do without a gown and veil, but she was still going to make this an event. Miriam always made the best of things, and he prized that trait in her. "Woman, I'm so glad you're mine."

❧

Admitting defeat didn't come easily. Miriam rolled over in her bed and stared at the white heap on the floor. She'd tried her best to stitch together the bodice while Reba whipped together the skirt. Even then, they'd come to the disappointing realization that if they had four other women here to spend all night sewing with them, the wedding gown wouldn't be finished.

Lord, You've blessed me with such a fine man. Help me to let go of little-girl dreams and be a woman who appreciates what she has instead of mourning the inconsequential things that might be missing.

She rolled out of bed and stoked the fire in her potbelly stove. Wedging the sadiron next to her teapot, she mentally listed what she'd need to get done in the next two hours. The men were supposed to have ham and a coffee cake she made last night—she didn't want to risk having Gideon catch a glimpse of her this morning. She'd iron her green paisley dress, then do Polly's hair. . . .

"Hey, Miriam! You awake?"

"Yes."

"Open up! I'm hauling over the tub."

She scrambled into her robe and eagerly opened the door so Paul could deliver that luxury. "Oh, thank you!"

Water splashed as he thumped the big galvanized tub down. "Glad to. Hang on. Titus is bringing a couple buckets of hot water to add." He grinned at her.

Self-consciously, she reached up and touched one of the rags in her hair. "It's a good thing the groom can't see the bride before the ceremony. Gideon would run for the hills if he saw me like this."

"He was teasing Polly about her rag curls just a few minutes ago."

Miriam gave him a startled look. "I didn't put her hair up."

"Dan did," Titus said as he arrived with the hot water. Laughter filled his voice. "If he weren't so grouchy this morning, we'd tease him unmercifully."

"Don't you dare. He was being a good daddy. I'm proud of him, and I'm going to tell him so just as soon as I see him."

Paul chortled. "You might want to wait until you see how Polly's hair turns out."

The brothers left, and Miriam gratefully slipped into the tub. She wished she had time to soak, but she still needed to iron her dress. Dried, powdered, and wearing everything except her dress, she laid the ironing board across her bed and draped the green paisley on it. Fingering the lace, she smiled. Gideon bought that lace for her. In fact, he bought the material, too, saying it would match her pretty eyes. It was the first compliment he'd paid her. The memory made the dress seem dearer.

Heavy footsteps sounded outside her doorstep. After a prolonged hesitation, someone knocked. Miriam slipped back into her robe and opened the door. "Daniel!"

He stood there, his face gaunt and eyes glinting with tears. "Hannah would have wanted you to have this." He shoved a bundle into her arms.

Miriam looked down. *Mama's wedding gown.* "Oh, Daniel—"

He cleared his throat. "I'm happy for Gideon. You'll make him a fine bride."

"You don't know how much it means to hear you say that."

"I can't be at the wedding. I can't see—"

Miriam pushed the dress back into his arms. "I'd rather have you there than wear the dress. You matter far more—"

"Don't ask that of me, Miriam. It's not just Hannah's gown. I can't listen to the vows." He shook his head as he rasped, "I just can't."

The anguish in his voice tore at her. Tears spilled from her eyes.

Daniel rasped, "Don't. Gideon's already furious that I'm not attending. If he knows I made you cry. . ." He hitched a shoulder.

"I understand. I'll make things right with Gideon, Daniel."

"I'll be at the reception when you have it." He shoved the dress into her arms again and wheeled around.

Miriam couldn't believe he'd opened Hannah's chest and suffered all of this pain to give her the wedding gown with his blessing. She whispered tearfully, "Thank you, Daniel."

He nodded and trudged away.

Lord, he hurts so badly. Ease his sorrow and show us how to help him through his grief. The Whites' buggy rolled up, drawing Miriam back to the fact that she needed to get ready. She shut the door and turned to iron the wedding gown.

Minutes later, Reba rapped on the door and let herself in. "Wonder of wonders, will you look at that! That bridal gown is exquisite."

"It was Mama's. Hannah wore it. Daniel is loaning it to me."

"That's a fine thing, indeed. Here. I'll set myself to doing the ironing. You fix your hair."

Miriam unwound the rags from her hair and started styling it. "I appreciate your help so much."

"Honey, that's what friends are for. My, this gown is lovely. The men are going to be pea green with envy that Gideon swept you off your feet."

Miriam smiled. "We get along well enough. They're all happy I'm marrying their brother."

"Dear, I know that. I mean all of the other men. Logan and Bryce rode out yesterday and spread the word. Everyone's still coming today for the nuptials."

"But I only made one little cake!"

Reba started laughing. "Wait 'til you see what Gideon did last night." Miriam gave her a questioning look, but Reba swished her hand in the air. "Don't ask me. You'll have to wait and find out for yourself."

Logan brought Polly over. Polly's hair resembled a jumble of giant watch springs, and the sash on her dress looked just as hopelessly twisted. Logan stuck a basket of flowers into Polly's hands. "Gideon picked these with her. He said they're for your hair."

Polly wiggled like an eager puppy. "I want some in my hair, too."

"We've got to do something about it," Reba murmured.

"Anything," Logan agreed, "would be an improvement."

"That's what Unca Titus said 'bout Unca Giddy's cupcakes." Polly stood on tiptoe and reached over her head. "He gots a big pile all stacked up this high."

Logan spluttered, spun away, and shut the door. His howling laughter still filtered into the cottage.

Reba got the giggles. "I guess the surprise is out. Maybe it's best you know before you see it, Miriam. It's the sorriest sight I've ever seen. That man and his brothers desperately need you."

"Gideon was trying to make today perfect." Miriam started combing Polly's hair into some semblance of order. Her heart overflowed. He was doing everything he could to turn this hurried event into something special. "He loves me."

"He's a fine man—one in a million," Reba agreed.

A short while later, Reba tucked one last flower into Miriam's hair, fussed to make sure the skirt hung just so, and scooted back to admire her. "Lovely. Just lovely! I'm going to go on out now."

Polly scrambled down from the chair over by the window. "They gots benches out there like for church. Lotsa men are here."

"It sounds as if everything's ready." Miriam retied Polly's sash and gave her a hug. "You're so pretty, Polly."

"Amazing what wonders a woman's touch can do." Laughter tinged Reba's voice. She took Polly by the hand, then looked at Miriam and asked, "Who's going to walk you down the aisle?"

"We talked it over, and I want Gideon to come claim me. There's no one present to give me away, and it just seems right to hold fast to his arm from the start."

Reba and Polly scooted out, and Miriam dabbed on a little perfume. *Lord, Thou art so generous. Thou knowest my heart and hast blessed me far beyond my wildest dreams. Thank Thee for Gideon and the love we share. Help me to be a good wife to him.*

A single, solid *thump* sounded. Gideon. It was his knock.

It's time.

She opened the door.

Gideon took a long, slow look at her—from the flowers in her hair, down her bridal gown, to the tips of her shoes. "Sweet pea, you make me believe in miracles."

"You take my breath away."

He winked. "Save enough to speak your vows, darlin'. There's nothing I want more in this world than for you to be mine."

"I love you, Gideon." She accepted the bouquet of wildflowers he handed her and stepped out to meet her future with him by her side.

A Letter To Our Readers

Dear Reader:

In order that we might better contribute to your reading enjoyment, we would appreciate your taking a few minutes to respond to the following questions. We welcome your comments and read each form and letter we receive. When completed, please return to the following:

Fiction Editor
Heartsong Presents
PO Box 719
Uhrichsville, Ohio 44683

1. Did you enjoy reading *One Chance in a Million* by Cathy Marie Hake?
   ❏ Very much! I would like to see more books by this author!
   ❏ Moderately. I would have enjoyed it more if

   _____
   _____
   _____

2. Are you a member of **Heartsong Presents**? ❏ Yes ❏ No
   If no, where did you purchase this book? _____
   _____

3. How would you rate, on a scale from 1 (poor) to 5 (superior), the cover design? _____

4. On a scale from 1 (poor) to 10 (superior), please rate the following elements.

   ____ Heroine   ____ Plot
   ____ Hero   ____ Inspirational theme
   ____ Setting   ____ Secondary characters

5. These characters were special because?_____

_____

_____

6. How has this book inspired your life?_____

_____

_____

7. What settings would you like to see covered in future
   Heartsong Presents books? _____

_____

_____

8. What are some inspirational themes you would like to see
   treated in future books? _____

_____

_____

9. Would you be interested in reading other **Heartsong
   Presents** titles? ❑ Yes ❑ No

10. Please check your age range:
        ❑ Under 18   ❑ 18-24
        ❑ 25-34   ❑ 35-45
        ❑ 46-55   ❑ Over 55

Name_____

Occupation _____

Address _____

City_____ State_____ Zip_____

SCRAPS OF LOVE

4 stories in 1

As long as women have been sewing, there have been boxes of scraps. The women of the Collins family have such a treasure box.

Tracie V. Bateman of Missouri gathered a team of authors, including Lena Nelson Dooley of Texas, Rhonda Gibson of New Mexico, and Janet Spaeth of North Dakota, to create this generational romance collection.

Historical, paperback, 352 pages, 5 ³⁄₁₆" x 8"

Heart♥song